INDISCREET MEMOIRS

ANONYMOUS

Carroll & Graf Publishers, Inc.
New York

Copyright © 1990 by Carroll & Graf Publishers, Inc
All rights reserved

First Carroll & Graf edition 1990

Carroll & Graf Publishers, Inc
260 Fifth Avenue
New York, NY 10001

ISBN: 0-88184-663-5

Manufactured in the United States of America

1

*T*HERE are moments when the hand of fate brushes one's brow with a gesture so meaningful that only a fool would ignore it.

So it was upon my leaving the cottage and returning home. My meeting and my conversation with Mrs. Hodge had aroused at first a hope in me. Now it seemed as if my mind were as a summer sky suddenly overcast by clouds.

I knew not the meaning of my depression, for I am rarely given to low spirits. Something has always happened to fill my mind, to divert me. On this occasion, however, no such fortune occurred. Retiring to my room I lay in the deepest despair. Only by the most determined efforts did I at last arouse myself and summon my maid, Mary.

2

She was new to me—a pleasant young girl of some seventeen years who always attended quietly and with the utmost obedience to my needs. In aspect we were not unlike, save that her face was rounder than my own.

"Bring me some Benedictine, Mary—my flask is empty."

"Yes, m'am." She curtsied and was gone. The quickness of her footsteps pleased me. Evidently she divined my mood and waited gazing down upon me while I sipped my first glass.

"My lady is unwell?"

"It will pass, Mary."

There was a dullness in my voice that communicated itself to her. I scarce knew my own mood. Summoning myself in spirit I asked her to prepare my bath and rose immediately upon her going in order to remove my dress.

It was then, perhaps, in the act of undressing that I found the key. My nudity was enticing still. Young as I was, my breasts showed their firm poise. My legs, tapering finely from my ankles up to well-turned calves, were flawless. My thighs bore a very slight plumpness such as I had found men admired. My bottom protruded with impertinence. My attractions were as ever.

I leaned against the glass of my stand mirror and cooled my brow. In but twenty-four hours, had I entered between the sheets with Jock, I might have made myself enceinte. The bulging of my belly for months thereafter would attract no man, least of all Lord Endover.

I was bored. There lay the other key to it. The boredom of marriage and the boredom of sharing my bed nightly with the same man were suddenly upon me. My conversation with Mrs. Hodge had been but a warning signal. I had sought escape in that which would do me the least good. I must get away.

I bathed quickly and perfumed myself well. A hunting reunion dinner had been arranged by Lord Endover for the following evening. The thought of it repelled me. A train to London would depart in two hours, as I learned. I decided to take it, and to take Mary with me. The idea of visiting London overwhelmed her.

"Oh, m'am!" was all she could seem to say. I attired her in one of my cloaks—a blue one—and a new pair of boots. She would have gazed at herself entranced for hours had I not bustled her out. Her figure being of similar slenderness to my own, the cloak fitted her admirably.

We were not long alone in our carriage. At the second station a man entered and disposed of his small baggage upon the rack opposite to us. He was of middle years and with rather a grim aspect. Unfolding *The Times*, he began to read in a manner that annoyed me. It was my mood, no doubt.

His topcoat, which he had not bothered to remove, was open. A considerable protrusion showed between his sturdy thighs where his breeches were drawn tight. Quite clearly I could see his balls and the thickness of the root above them.

I nudged Mary and said something to her softly. Incredulous at my words she blushed deeply and giggled. Even so she took as close a look as I had. *The Times* lowered itself slowly.

"You spoke, Madam?"

"Something which does not concern you, sir."

I replied coolly yet there was no escaping a latent mischief in my eyes which he clearly read.

A chuckle escaped him—a quite unexpected sound. The wheels of the train rattled over the rails in the growing dusk. The countryside flashed past us. We had a full half an hour to the next station.

"That of which you spoke, Madam, concerns me much.

It is an instrument of the greatest convenience that has also pleasured many."

The Times was laid aside. He rose. His topcoat was quickly discarded. The protrusion in his breeches was now even bolder. That which had been but a root appeared to have become a small branch. A distinct trembling came from Mary who clutched my arm.

"You flatter yourself, no doubt. And pray of what instrument do you speak?"

I asked the question boldly. His air of insolence amused me. While Mary uttered a gasp, he crudely unbuttoned his breeches and displayed to our eyes a shaft of considerable girth, its head rosy above the veined column.

"Sir! how dare you! Oh, pray show it not to my servant —she is a girl of great innocence."

Indeed that appeared the case, for Mary had covered her eyes. I suspected her of peeping nevertheless through the fingers of her gloves.

"And you, Madam?"

His hands were strong. Before I knew his immediate intention I was drawn up from my seat to feel the throbbing of his hard monster against me.

"Pray! Oh pray do not!"

Groping the back of my skirt he had raised it already. I wondered rather at Mary's countenance as first my thighs and then my bottom were displayed closely to her in all their nudity in such circumstances.

"Ah! you devil!"

I endeavoured to twist from his grasp. The very movement was my undoing. The rattling of the train over points made me stumble in such wise that my gloved hand encountered his rampant limb. His eyes glowed.

"You shall both taste it."

At his declaration I affected a shriek which was echoed

behind me from Mary. In the same instant I felt myself spun about and flung half over her so that my face rested on her shoulder. The nudity of my lower half, decorated only by my gartered stockings, offered a perfect target for his endeavours. By seeming to wrestle fiercely I prevented Mary from rising. In the next moment the crest of his swollen limb was presented to my nether lips.

"Oh, for shame, sir!"

Mary fell sideways under my weight, I being forced to bend down further upon her. In the melee my hand encountered her knee which the rising of her skirt had exposed.

"Oh, m'am!"

A groaning behind me sounded. No doubt the lips of my slit were succulent to his nut which inserted itself but an inch in the most teasing of manners. I wriggled my hips suavely and by pretence of struggling managed to absorb a full half of the rampant thing.

"Ah! how rough, how wicked you are!"

My flushed face pressed its velvety cheek against Mary's. By chance my lips encountered the corner of her mouth.

"How tight you are! What bliss! What a silken interior —what luscious cheeks!"

"You must not! Ah, take it out!"

Had he done so I would have been left at a high pitch of frustration for his tool now was embedded fully within and in such a manner that I could not help but squeeze my distended lips upon it.

The swaying of the train assisted both our endeavours. With fervent sounds of happiness he began to work his thing back and forth in my grotto. My bottom bounced against his belly. He breathed hard and fast. I continued my thrusting as if trying to dismount him, though my sinuous movements served only to excite us both further as I could tell by the increased throbbing of his embedded member. At every push his balls, each three times the size of a large plum, smacked against my nether cheeks. Mary lay full beneath me, her legs dangling upon the floor of the carriage. My mouth was buried in her neck. I affected gasps of dismay while groping her thighs, as if trying to take purchase upon something.

"Oh!" she moaned again and again as if she too were enjoying the thrusts of his piston which had by now worked up a froth in me. His hands sought to caress my thighs, toying with the curls of my mount. Squeezing rapturously I spurted my pleasure, dousing his shaft which flashed ever faster.

"Delicious witch, you are coming! What skin, what buttocks, what legs—ah, what rapture!"

"Stop him, oh pray!"

I rolled my bottom avidly. Such lewd pleasures almost always excite me most. I was at a high pitch of pleasure. My right knee rested against the bared thigh of Mary whose flushed features perspired against mine. Groping as if wildly I exposed both her thighs. She shrieked and made to cover herself but was unable to force her hand down between us.

"Raise your bottom! I am coming!"

I obeyed as if helpless to do otherwise. My sobs resounded. The moisture of my lips passed across those of Mary's. Their sweet taste and their softness entranced me. I had never kissed a girl before during the act. The sensuousness was exquisite. I longed for her to pass her tongue into my mouth, but instead the foolish girl twisted her face aside. Her cunny being uncovered showed a fine dark brown bush that added to the endeavours of my assailant.

Bending far over me he attempted to grope her. There

was a further shriek from beneath me. By subterfuge I kept her knees apart with my own.

The stabbing of his rod seemed endless. I longed to feel his spurts. He was a long time about his pleasure yet enjoying every second of it. Of a sudden his reaching hand succeeded in cupping Mary's slit. She moaned and bucked —a prisoner beneath me.

"Ah! I am dousing you! How luscious you are! What a hot bottom!"

My eyes screwed up with pleasure, though he could not see it. Just beneath my vision I could see his fingers working about Mary's plump little grotto. Her hips jerked, her eyes rolled. Her pleasure, though secondary to my own, was obviously great.

Sliding both my legs down as if in an effort to escape the deluge, I straightened both legs and ground my bottom cheeks into him in an invitation he could not resist. A violent pulsing of his shaft within me and the first hot jet flooded me, to be followed by another and another while his entire frame trembled with bliss.

Truly he had expended his all. With a last murmur of satisfaction he held it full in me for a long moment and then withdrew the long thick weapon. Affecting tears I cast myself down upon the seat away from Mary and hid my face. It was my first such bout in front of a servant. I wondered at her thoughts even as I wondered at my own daring.

Yet I had dissimilated well. Calling him the worst of brutes as he sank down again in exceedingly limp state, she covered herself and did her best to comfort me, while drawing the veil of my skirt over my naked bottom.

"I shall tell the Station Master!"

My words appeared to alarm him.

"Madam, I beg you not! It was an act of foolishness—

of lust, yes, but your beauty overwhelmed me. I will do anything, anything!"

I rose and attempted as best I could to adjust my bonnet. Mary's hands assisted me. Her expression was sweet and concerned.

"M'am, there will be such trouble!" His face was wild with anguish. I had acted out my part better than I thought. No doubt he had thought his strength had completely overcome me. So great had been his effusion that it trickled down my thighs.

"That you should have thought of before your rude assault, sir. At the least there shall be recompense. Open your wallet!"

The startled manner in which he obeyed caused me almost to laugh aloud. In a moment his bulging purse was presented. I took it from his hands. Counting within I found notes from five pounds to fifty in value.

"It is my servant who shall be recompensed."

I extracted two ten pound notes. Under the guise of fumbling I took also two to the value of fifty pounds each and concealed them in my glove. The subterfuge amused me. I needed not the money but he would forever wonder where they had gone since I flourished the other two visibly before placing them in Mary's hand.

Such wealth she had never seen before.

"Take them, Mary—he has frightened you to death, a virgin as you are. No doubt the authorities would have much to say to him if this were known."

His visage was crumpled. I tossed the wallet back in his lap. His member hung like a huge thick worm. Following my apparently disdainful glance he quickly covered himself. The next station was nigh upon us. The engine began to slow.

Of a sudden he leapt up and seized his baggage, casting

the most apprehensive glances down upon me. I returned him my coldest stare. In any other circumstances, without the presence of Mary, I might have enjoyed a second bout.

The gas lamps along the platform flooded our carriage with light. Scarcely waiting for the train to stop he opened the door, leapt out, and was gone. His intended destination would not see him this night, I thought. In all probability he would hide in some nearby hotel in craven alarm.

Upon his going, Mary immediately drew down the blinds lest we be disturbed again. I affected a regal air and drew her to me.

"Do not be frightened too much, Mary."

"No m'am. Oh, you were so brave! How you truly fought! What a vile beast he was!"

Her gloved hand still clutched the notes as if she did not believe in their existence. They represented twenty times more than she had ever seen in her life.

"Such men exist, but others are kinder, Mary. You will do well to clothe yourself nicely now—at his expense. How scared you must have been, poor thing."

I kissed her, seeking again the corner of her mouth. She flushed a trifle but did not resist.

"No one must ever know."

"No, m'am. It shall be a secret, that I promise. Oh, what a big one he had!"

I smiled at her words and pressed her to me. Her skin was fresh and as smooth as velvet, as that of country girls often is.

"Are you a virgin, Mary? Did it frighten you? Ah, the rude fellow spilled so much in me. I need a kerchief."

"M'am, I will do it, permit me. Lie back."

I did so. She raised my skirt, tucking it beneath my bottom. The sperm glistened still on my thighs, around my bush and along the tops of my stockings. Her nostrils twitched at the scent of it as she wiped me dry. Impetuously I pressed her lips down upon my thigh.

"How sweet you are, Mary! Are you truly virgin?"

Her flustered eyes rose to mine. I adjusted my dress and sat up. The milky taste of my skin, combined with the scent of the male sperm, was still upon her lips.

"No, m'am—I was come upon, even like as you. In the shed it were. A rude fellow that was working with my father. He had me at his will. Oh, how I screamed and cried! Nothing stopped him. He was mad of lust for me he said. I suffered even as you did. His big thing was right in me. I was on my back in the straw. Nothing could save me."

"Did he spend in you?"

"He were beginning to. I could feel it. It were warm like thick milk or curd. He was groaning and saying things I couldn't understand. Then my father come upon us and he were out in a flash, his thing all stiff and the stuff still jerking out of it. My father gave him a belt and he run off. We never saw him again."

"What happened then?"

I was trembling inwardly with excitement. I placed my arm around her shoulders. My expression was one of great solicitousness. I kissed her brow.

"My father, m'am, he were real angry. Said as how I had invited it. Took me indoors, he did, and smacked my bottom hard. I howled and kicked. He would not believe me. My bottom was right red. Then he took sorrow on me and sat me up on his lap and kissed me, saying he were carried away."

"What a treasure he must think you, Mary."

"Yes, m'am. I thought I were truly wicked and perhaps I had invited it—asked for it like. I should never have gone in the shed with him. I told father so. He kissed me again and said he understood."

"That was nice. It is always best to confess and to be understood. Was that all?"

"No, m'am. It were near the end of day. Father said as we didn't need to work in the fields again till morning. He said as my bottom was smarting and wriggling so on his lap he would soothe me. Oh, m'am!"

Mary hid her face in my shoulder.

"He soothed you nicely, I am sure."

"I didn't mean it, nor he. I swear to that."

"Mean what? Am I not your confidante—your friend now? Shall you not tell me? You have seen how rudely I was handled. I can feel it in me still."

"Father said to go on the bed and took my dress off. I wore nothing beneath 'cept my stockings, and they was rough. I lay on my tummy while he soothed my hot bottom with a little oil he brought. It felt funny. I tried to lie still but I couldn't."

"Then he kissed you again to make you feel better?"

My excitement was rising so much that I could feel my heart pounding.

"M'am, you won't say—you won't tell?"

"Go on, Mary."

"It weren't my fault, nor his. I was excited after what happened. When he rolled me over and kissed me I did not know what to do. He said I were real lovely and kissed my nipples. I started and tried to get up but he pressed me back. Only a minute, he said. I could see by his face that he felt funny. He got his thing out, all stiff it were, and put it in my hand. Only to rub it and feel nice, he said."

"Did you? Were you kind to him, Mary?"

"I rubbed it. I were rare excited the way he were kissing me, though I knew I mustn't be. Then he pushed it up and down faster in my hand and shot it out all over me. He gave a big sigh and then half fell on me, rubbing it on my belly. I was sticky and wet. I knew he didn't mean to."

"No, of course, Mary. Did he again?"

"No, m'am, I think he would've done, but my mother were always about, and my sisters. A week later I went into service. I had a real cry when I left."

It was a sweet story, though there are dolts enough who would consider it immoral. Had he been fully in rut as my assailant had been no doubt the story would have been coarser.

"One cannot blame him. You are very pretty, Mary."

The words diverted her.

"Oh, m'am, do you think so?"

"Put your money away, for we are nearing Victoria Station now."

We ascended. A porter fetched our baggage. Mary's eyes were like saucers. She had never seen such a huge station before. Our trunks preceded us on a trolley. In but a few moments we were ensconced in a carriage. A feeling of relief seized me. I had done the right thing.

With an uprising of pleasure in my heart we bore towards Eaton Square.

2

*T*HE hour was late upon our arrival. John came out to take my trunks. His eyes glowed upon seeing me. Sippett hovered nervously in the doorway, her glance as slyly curious as ever.

I placed Mary in her charge. Papa, as I learned, was at one of his clubs. It was uncertain as to whether he intended to return that night.

I took a bath while Mary unpacked. Her delight at finding herself in London was evident. To my pleasure she returned immediately to her quiet way, concealing everything of what had passed.

In my boudoir I donned but a light silk robe and renewed my stockings. Their sensuous feel and tightness about my thighs always pleases me. John brought me up a light supper of chicken. I kept Mary by me until he had retreated. I wanted none of him that night. The man on the train had excited me rather than fulfilled me. Mary's narrative had stirred me also. I knew what I wanted.

"Have a message taken to the Carlton Club and others. Lord L. is to know that I have returned."

I had quite forgotten that she knew nothing of these places. Mary's eyes were wide and anxious. Her obvious apprehension about displeasing me touched me.

"Tell Sippett the message. She will arrange it. Be sure that I have liqueurs sent up—and a few chocolates. I shall not need you again tonight, Mary, nor am I to be disturbed again after this."

"No, m'am."

She had had her own excitement for the night and would dwell much in her bed on how to spend her little fortune. I intended to guide her in that. She could yet play such roles as were already weaving in my mind.

The chocolates, when brought, tasted delicious. They were of the dark variety that I like. Their taste combined well with the liqueurs. Alone at last I lay back with my robe open and considered anew my future. It would be as well to let Lord Endover know that I had merely decided upon London for a few weeks. Events could then take their own run. There was one person to whom I wished to confess, and that was Papa.

An hour endured before he arrived. He had been at the last club the messenger had tried. His delight upon seeing me again was exceeding. Plainly he was fit and well again. Disappointment showed upon his features as, with my robe sheathed fully about me, I proffered him only my cheek to kiss.

"We must talk, Papa."

His eyes grew concerned. He drew up a chair while I lounged on the edge of the bed and toyed with my chocolates. We partook of a glass of Cointreau together.

"My Eveline is in trouble?"

"No, Papa, I think not. The world about me is rather in trouble for it does not always fit me. Do not be alarmed, pray. My health is excellent—Lord Endover is equally well. It is marriage, Papa. It does not suit me."

His hand clasped my own, brown as it was over my white skin.

"I feared as such, though I dared not say. You are bored —*distrait*?"

The concern in his eyes was expressive. Leaning forward off the edge of the bed I looped one arm over his shoulders and laid my head there.

"Am I horrible to say it, Papa?"

"My dear, no. You always speak the truth. I have never known you do other. Lord Endover knows of this?"

"No. I left upon his absence. I could not wait to face explanations. How boring, too, they can be. I intend to stay for a few weeks and so to let matters pass. We shall see what he will do upon my absence. He has of course his clubs, his shooting, his regimental friends. I am not his entire world."

"Not as you are mine, Eveline."

"Oh, Papa, is that true? Is that still true?"

I shifted my head. Our mouths met and lingered. The sweetness of my breath made his frame tremble. In the middle of our embrace he rose up from his chair and pressed me upon my back so that my legs dangled over the edge of the bed.

"It will ever be true, my pet. Your beauty, your charm, the delights of your form—all excite and fulfill me."

"I shall be your little Eveline again—your own one. Would you like that?"

"More than anything on earth."

Bent full over me as he was, our lips met anew. I protruded my tongue—it met his own. Thrills of pure delight shot through my veins. Seeking down between us I found with my fingers the rod of his shaft which had already awoken. Unfastening the buttons while our tongues played ever more passionately I succeeded in clasping the stiff, fleshy tool. It throbbed in my palm. I felt his balls, their heaviness—full of love's milk for me.

"Let me suck it first—lie back, Papa."

I slipped from under him and, standing, cast off my robe.

"Ah! my love! My Eveline!"

"I am naked for you, Papa, save for my stockings—the sheerest silk. Is that not what you want?"

Before he could answer I bent my head and clasped his stiff member anew. The rosy purplish head glowed its delight. A hollow groan sounded from him. I parted my lips about it and descended them slowly until a five full inches of the shaft was enclosed in my warm mouth. My saliva moistened it. I slid my lips luringly up and down. His throaty cries were my delight.

I freed it from my mouth for but a moment.

"Do not come, Papa—your Eveline will suck it otherwise in a moment between her thighs."

"Sweet child! Ah, your delicious mouth—what warmth and wetness. How firm your breasts, how luscious your bottom and thighs."

"You shall have them all in a moment, Papa. Ah! you naughty man! you have come a little!"

It was but the first trickle on my tongue, yet it warned me

of his increasing excitement. I relinquished my delicious task, leaving his member proud and upstanding.

"Papa, you must be naked, too!"

I threw myself on the bed, my legs languidly apart, the better that he could relish the sight of the peeping of my lovelips in their nest. Sinewy and strong, he cast himself down half upon me, his tool throbbing on my belly. Our tongues enjoined once more. I dallied lightly with his shaft. Desire was rich in me. I felt a freedom that I had not known since my wedding day.

"Oh, Papa—have your little girl, your own one!"

He was full upon me like a lion. My legs spread full. For a tremulous moment the swollen nut of his tool pressed upon the curls of my mount. Then with a mutual gasp and moan he was within. A single thrust sufficed for the root to bury itself to the full. His hands cupped my bottom. My stockinged calves twined themselves tightly about his hips. The dangling weight of his balls swung against my nether cheeks.

The pleasure was such that neither of us spoke for a long minute. Papa's nostrils flared with lust. He saw perhaps the devil in my eyes.

"It is incest, Papa. Are we not wicked? How exquisite it feels! Ah, move your big thing—make it work—make me come!"

I was almost beside myself with the sensuousness of the act. My buttocks wriggled enticingly on his palms, made his monstrous thing churn about within me as he thrust it back and forth. My nipples, stiff with desire, rubbed beneath his chest.

I closed my eyes, wishing to blot out everything save the sensations I was being accorded. Papa's lips brushed my ear. We exchanged broken words of lust. The faint squelching of his piston working back and forth in my slit excited us both exceedingly. I squeezed upon it tightly, though it filled me almost as much as had that of the man in the train.

"Give me your mouth, your tongue, Eveline! Ah, my own sweet daughter, how prettily you do it! Work your adorable bottom more! Let me part the cheeks and play with it."

"Oh, yes, Papa, yes! Your Eveline has no secrets from you. Enter your finger there—AH! how wicked, how exciting! Come in me, come—empty your balls, Papa!"

My rosette yielded to his finger even as my slit had yielded to his shaft. The sensation was divine. I implored more. My eyes rolled up in my head so that Papa swore afterwards that he feared I was fainting. Indeed I almost was—from pleasure. Ramming me vigourously his finger entered my bottomhole to the first knuckle. The dual experience was beyond belief. I rocked and sobbed. I was beside myself. Twice I spattered his indriving tool with love's essence before the spurting streams of sperm leapt powerfully from his stiff root.

"F . . f . . . f . . . fill me, Papa! Ah, your sperm —how strongly you discharge!"

Violent quivers shook us. His finger worked miracles in my bottom which had eased and opened to receive it. I came again even as the last, more feeble shoots jetted from his tool. We sank inert. His finger removed itself. I felt a curious emptiness there. I wriggled slyly to hold him in me still. His thighs tremored upon my own.

"How gloriously pretty you are!" he groaned. His face sank on my shoulder. I stroked and soothed him.

"You must stay, Papa. Come, get between the sheets with me. We shall not be disturbed. Your Eveline is greedy for it tonight."

The flabby member slipped upon my thigh. Its wet nose rubbed against the top of my stocking. Kicking down the covers with my feet, I breathed a sigh of satisfaction and turned over. The sheets enfolded us. Without speaking I began rubbing my bottom against his tool.

I had no regrets. Lord Endover seemed to me already but a shadowy figure. Would that I had but dreamed my marriage. I trembled within myself at the thought that in a moment of hopeful carelessness I might have cast myself beneath Jock and displayed thereafter little more than a swollen belly.

Papa's hands slipped beneath my armpits to weight and fondle my gourds. Their stiff nipples stirred against his thumbs. I enticed him by rolling movements of my bottom. Dearly as I loved him, it was his sense of lechery that I sought. In such moments as this it perfectly matched my own.

"Poor Papa, you are not like Charlemagne—you have but one daughter with whom to dally."

My bottom was ever urgent. I desired him again. I doubt not that he knew it.

"My Eveline alone suffices. Raise your upper leg high, my pet—higher. Now I can feel your darling slit. How pulpy it is!"

"With your sperm, naughty Papa. It trickles down my thighs—you can feel. Ah! put your finger in—now tickle my button! Would you not have two—two daughters? What lustfulness you would enjoy!"

"You would permit it—if you had had a sister?"

I squirmed and laughed. I turned about in his embrace to face him. My palm sought his balls and weighed them. We were indeed in a rare mood of love's pleasure. Already his penis stirred anew with the thoughts I had induced in him.

"How pretty it would be to watch, Papa. Her bottom would wriggle on your palms with pleasure. AH! Papa!"

I had excited him as at no other time. With a growl of lust

he was upon me. I began to struggle—emulating that which I had described.

"No, you must not! Oh! your naughty big thing!"

His shaft seemed thicker and longer than ever. Probing the curls of my already spermed slit, it entered slowly. I received it. My belly joined to his. Papa's lips sucked upon my stiff nipples. The pleasure was exquisite.

"Divine little witch that you are, my pet—it would be as you say. Would you not coax and persuade her?"

"Of course," I said hotly. I squeezed lovingly upon his member which was fully sheathed. Our tongues played a fine game together. We exchanged a thousand obscenities between kisses. Our words and our imaginations knew no bounds. Papa took longer upon it this time. His strokes, slow and powerful, filled and refilled my slit. My breath, perfumed with liqueurs and chocolates, intoxicated him. Cupping my bottom in his fervent endeavours, Papa gripped and held the cheeks apart. The sensation of so being held was delightful. Our breathing came coarsely.

"Your finger in my bottom!" I implored. I had never sought it there before. A madness of eroticism had seized me.

Papa's finger entered my rose. The feeling combined with his member moving in my more pliable sheath made me sob with pleasure. I worked upon his finger. I urged it further in. Our salivas mingled.

"Two! We shall both have two!" I gasped.

Whether he understood or not I do not know, but his loins quickened. The interior of my vagina gripped him spongily. I was free. I knew it now through a dazzling mist of pleasures. I recalled Mary and her confession. She would be easily converted. Papa would have a double pleasure.

"How tight your bottom is—how delicious, my pet!"

I jerked my bottom impetuously. The smooth movements

back and forth of his finger in my most secret orifice pleased me almost as much as that of his tool in my slit.

"Fuck me, Papa!"

The words burst from my lips before I knew it. It was never a term I had used before, but now the utter licentiousness of the moment called it forth. The effect upon him was electric.

"Ah, Eveline! what an exquisite fuck you are! I must have your bottom soon!"

His come began to shoot forth immediately. The streams were longer and thicker than I expected. I was thoroughly doused. The thought that I might receive a similar injection in my bottom from another cock at the same time brought me to a thrilling climax. My lovelips tightened like a clam about his shaft. Groaning together, we threshed our last.

Then a knock sounded—not upon my door but below in the hall! In the stillness of the night we could not help but hear it. The noise came upon us like a thunderclap. We clutched one another, frozen in our lewd posture.

"My God, dearest, we shall be undone!"

"Hide, Papa, hide, lest a servant enter. In the closet, quickly!"

A perfect comedy ensued. Uncorking both his finger and his member at the same time with quite a plop, Papa scrambled off me and cast himself into my wardrobe.

There were noises below. Throwing my gown around me once more, I hastily smoothed the sheet and cast the covers upon it. A timid knock sounded at my door whereat I hastened to close the door of the wardrobe.

"What is it?"

"Your Uncle Edward and your cousin Emma, m'am."

I glanced at my clock. It was a quarter to midnight—an unconscionable hour for visitors.

"I will dress and come down, Sippett."

"There is no reply from Lord L.'s room, m'am."

"I doubt it not—his Lordship is exceedingly tired. On no account will you disturb him again."

"No, m'am."

I drew my gown tightly about me and repaired the disorder of my hair. Preparing to descend I reopened the door of my wardrobe for a moment and gazed at Papa.

He was indeed very limp.

3

*D*ISMAYED as I was at the untoward nature of the interruption, I was yet intrigued.

Uncle Edward and his family lived in Herefordshire. They were not often to be found in London except during the Season. Entering the drawing room I found him, bluff and bucolic as ever, drinking port. My cousin Emma, still bonneted, sat beside him as if ill at ease.

Emma was then eighteen, a girl of slightly round countenance whom I had always found too quiet and secretive for my tastes. I adhere to secrets myself, but Emma's I felt sure were of an exceedingly dull or sly type.

Immediately upon entering I became aware of the flimsiness of my gown and the fact that I wore nothing beneath save my stockings. A parting of the folds permitted my uncle to feast his eyes for a moment upon the legs that revealed themselves even to my thighs. Emma blushed. I frowned at her and sat down quickly, my uncle rising and falling again like a puppet.

"Father is exhausted or he would have come down."

"My dear Eveline, yes. I feared much to disturb you at this hour. A thousand apologies. I was minded to bring Emma to town for dress fittings. The hotels it appears are full. We have wandered around many, have we not, Emma?"

She nodded. Her eyes were slightly small but her nose straight and pleasing. She had a little mouth almost forming a perfect Cupid's bow.

"Have you not drunk, Emma?"

"A glass of water only, Cousin."

I hated being termed that. I felt sure that she knew it. It was the normal parlance but belonged to more common folk.

"We shall accommodate you most gladly, Uncle. Have you eaten?"

They had dined well, it appeared. My curiosity was further aroused in that my aunt at last had not accompanied them. I asked if she were well. In order, as it seemed, to accommodate himself better to my questions my uncle moved his chair around the table a little. To his undoubted dismay I kept the folds of my gown together.

My aunt, it appeared, was indisposed but was anxious that upon attaining her eighteenth birthday, as she just had, Emma should not be rivalled in her attire by other young ladies of the district. They were to have called upon us on the morrow in any event. My further tête-à-têtes with Papa might have to be postponed as indeed might any other adventures in which I wished to enter. It was a considerable annoyance. I had seen my uncle but a few times since my return from France. He did not please me entirely, though he was obviously a man of some vigour. His lecherousness was obvious in his frequent glances at my legs and at the rather low nature of the neckline of my gown.

Since they had feasted and wined, I had no need to detain them downstairs. Their rooms were quickly accommodated. I bid both the best of nights and kissed both dutifully. My uncle's lips fell upon my own, though I had offered him my cheek.

The house was quiet again. I saw to it that Sippett was back in her room on the fourth floor before descending to my own. The wardrobe trembled distinctly as I opened it. Papa believed himself to be uncovered—as truly he was. We spoke in whispers, sitting together on my bed. At least some forty minutes must pass before he could feel free to go into the corridor and enter his own room.

I removed my gown once more and lay back with my thighs parted. A certain turgidness in Papa's member made it evident to my eyes that he was not beyond arousal again.

Smiling at him and placing my fingers to my lips I began to toy with his shaft. In but five minutes as I dangled my legs over the edge of the bed he was upon me. The bed creaked slightly. The door was locked. We were at our pleasure.

Papa took so long about it—to my distinct pleasure—that it was a full fifteen minutes before the final spasms of desire shook him. By then I had spilled my own lovejuice several times.

It was the first time that we had enjoyed three bouts together. His virility astonished me. We were both, it seemed, renewed.

26

In the morning I dressed myself a trifle more sedately than is my wont. I intended Emma not to rival me in her gowns. Neither did I wish to display more than I needed to my uncle. By mid-morning Papa had engaged him at his club. A boredom settled upon me. Emma was evidently taking her time in visiting the dress establishments.

An idea came to me that was as perverse as it was enjoyable. I would take her, I said, to the shop of M. Dalmaine, my own bootmaker. I needed in any event some new boots for myself.

Emma assented with far less enthusiasm than I would have displayed. I was minded to shake her. Instead I lent her the softest of my tones and the sweetest of my cousinly smiles. The sooner she was outfitted the sooner we would be rid of them.

M. Dalmaine was overjoyed to make my acquaintance again—as well he might be. He led us into his *atelier* behind the shop and a little above it. I could sense a certain frustration in him as he produced his latest fashions from a glass case. I surmised that the presence of Emma had put him out of countenance. On my previous visit I had "driven him to the mad" as he expressed it. His big member had foamed in my grotto in tribute.

Now, however, I saw the cause of his unease. The door which led further into the house opened to admit a lady of some thirty-five and of considerable attractions. It was his wife, Monique. She had returned from a stay in France. Greeting us both, her eyes stayed for a moment in mine.

"I have something of special interest to show you, Mademoiselle. If you care to accompany me while your pretty friend is being attended to?"

"Of course."

I left Emma gazing after me, perched on a chair while M. Dalmaine knelt before her to measure her feet. How much else he would try to measure I wondered with amusement as I was led within a small but comfortable sitting room.

"Something special—*oui*, Mademoiselle. I bring from Paris. Soon we copy for special young ladies here."

I gazed down at what she presented to me from a large box. I was flattered, after all, to be considered "special." The boots were as none I had ever seen before. They were of a length that would encompass not only my calves and knees but at least half my thighs as well.

"They must be extremely uncomfortable, surely?"

"They are for private occasions only. One soon becomes used to them. See! I have a pair on myself."

Madame Dalmaine laid the boots down and stepped back. Smiling with a slight air of shyness she raised her skirts. Her calves were well-turned, her thighs smooth and of a perfect whiteness, showing not a blemish. The soft leather boots hugged her pretty limbs to perfection and were held with thin leather ties, which emerged from loopholes, midway up her thighs.

The vision was entrancing. I had not believed one could walk in them. In this I was wrong. The leather was so thin and supple that movement was not impeded. Madame walked back and forth, still holding her skirts up, and then approached me.

"Feel how soft they are, Mademoiselle."

I placed my hand upon her nearest leg, feeling with my fingertips how the warmth of her flesh came through the leather. A certain silence obtained as I moved my hand upwards. I encountered no resistance.

"Yes, very soft, Madame Dalmaine."

"Yes? You think so?"

My fingers scouted around the rim of the boot. The surface above was silky. Her skirts raised themselves higher. Beneath the line of my vision, without obviously lowering my glance, I could perceive a fine dark bush of curls at the junction of her thighs.

"You would like, Mademoiselle?"

"You may measure me."

I made my voice slightly curt. I did not intend to entertain, but to be entertained. Madame Dalmaine nodded, smiled, and knelt before me as I sat. Her hands lifted my skirts delicately. A murmur of appreciation broke from her lips. My patterned white silk stockings attracted her gaze as did the paleness of my thighs above.

I parted my legs and waited. A small sigh perhaps escaped me.

"Your husband has my measurements, Madame."

"Have you his, Mademoiselle?"

Before I could think to reply I felt both my calves lifted. In a second my knees dangled over her shoulders.

"Ah, what perfection, Mademoiselle! What delicious curls, what pretty pouting lips! *Donnes-le-moi!*"

I had never felt another woman's tongue between my thighs before. The sensation was unexpected and rapturous. The tip of her tongue licked upwards, first parting the lips which the journey in the carriage had already made moist. Seeking further it sought my bud. I husked a cry and tightened my knees over her shoulders. My clitoris erected itself immediately. Bending forward as best I could I seized her head and drew her lips in full contact with the lips of my cunny.

"Lick within also!"

Her muffled assent came to me. I sank down slightly in the chair and eased my bottom forward. Her hands cupped the naked cheeks as Papa's had done, but she made no attempt to draw them apart.

I murmured and twisted. Her tongue licked and lapped, sometimes darting within my folds like a warm snake and, at the others, twirling about my pleasure bud. Swirling mists of desire seized me. Ideas I had never entertained before spilled in my head.

"Faster! lick faster!"

I was coming already. Delicious spasms seized me. The skin of my belly rippled. Straightening my legs forward over her bowed shoulders I spilled a fine, salty rain over her tongue and lips and heaved my bottom frantically. No man's tongue would be as subtle or agile as this. The pleasures of Lesbos—those with which I had but briefly flirted with Mary in the railway carriage—captivated me as surely as that greedily darting tongue. Bubblings of delight came from my mouth. A second spasm shook me and I again inundated her mouth. Then I quivered and lay still.

Releasing my legs from her shoulders gently, Madame Dalmaine rose to her feet. For a second or two I seemed not conscious of my surroundings, then I came to myself and sat up. I knew not whether to be pleased or cross with her at her impertinence. Perhaps something of this showed in my expression, for she stepped back and thrust down her own skirts. The slightly submissive gesture pleased me. Having ravished me, she was experiencing some doubt and shyness.

I rose. Her eyes implored me. I embraced her. My lips tasted the musky salty taste upon her own.

"Did I not give Mademoiselle pleasure?"

For a moment I did not answer. I placed my hands upon her hips and felt their fullness. Still unspeaking I moved them about to feel the undoubted moon of her bottom. The cheeks were firm and resilient and not over-large.

"I shall see you again."

I maintained an evenness of tone that would leave her in some little wondering. She had pleasured me more than she knew. I reentered the *atelier* and there found Emma waiting in some dismay at my absence.

"I have ordered a pair of long boots from your wife."

"Yes, Mademoiselle."

He affected, too, not to see my wedding ring which I had forgotten to remove, as I had intended to do for my own purposes.

"I shall return for a fitting in two weeks."

The carriage awaited us still. I entered before Emma who seated herself with bright cheeks beside me. It was evident that she was choking to say something.

"Oh, Eveline, that man—he felt my thighs!"

My expression did not alter. I had had my own felt in a wise she would know little about. A warm moisture lingered about my cunny still. It was an experience I intended to renew.

"I am sure he had need to, Emma. Did you order some nice boots?"

"Oh yes—two pairs of black and two of brown."

"Well, then, you are content. I am sure your Papa will be quite busy in town, Emma. I shall escort you myself on your errands. This afternoon we shall order some little corsets for you—just for your waist, of course, so that you are fully tightened. It displays your hips and bottom better."

Her blush amused me. Perhaps it was the first real moment of interest that I showed in her. The word "bottom" was evidently considered impolite, which surprised me. Rural folk are often coarser than town people. They observe more frequently the farm animals and their couplings. We lunched at the house alone. I saw to it that Emma took rather more wine than she would otherwise have done. It would loosen her a little from her rather prim and affected manner.

By three-thirty we had entered a discreet little establishment just off Regent Street. I had learned of it vaguely from one of Lord Endover's female friends. The most delicate and fetching of waist corsets were made there, she had said.

The entrance was but a vestibule. Within it stood a small showcase displaying three extremely pretty corsets in white, black, and rose-pink. Another door of frosted glass faced us and there we entered, to be received by a gentleman of somewhat military appearance and elegant attire. The small reception room was otherwise empty. Emma stood behind me. No doubt the fact that M. Dalmaine had felt her thighs had made her nervous.

"The ladies wish to be measured?"

I afforded him a slightly frosty look.

"There is no female assistant present?"

"Alas, Madame, no. Both our ladies are unfortunately indisposed. Allow me to introduce myself. I am Clarence Partinger, the designer of such poor articles as we sell."

His manner amused me. His voice was graceful but clipped. The small moustache he affected suited him, as did the cravat he wore which was tucked neatly into his puce waistcoat.

"I fear, sir, it would be improper for us to be measured by a gentleman. We shall return another time. Come, Emma."

"Madame!"

His voice sounded fraught. I turned.

"There is no need for you, Madame, to remove your attire. I have but to take three measurements and with these I can make my estimates. Having then chosen your styles, you and your companion may return for a proper fitting with one of our ladies."

I read his eyes too well even though he endeavoured to cloud his expression.

"Very well—if it is as simple as that. My cousin and I are of the same size, hence you have only need to measure me."

He bowed. Emma took a chair and picked up a copy of the *Englishwoman's Domestic Magazine*. Guided by my host I entered another room which was literally walled with ornately framed mirrors. To one side were more display cases revealing what seemed to me to be even smaller corsets. Along an opposite wall was a couch covered in red velvet. It had a somewhat used look. Mr. Partinger took up a tape measure. I raised my arms.

"The first measurement, Madame, around your waist. Ah! how delightfully slender it is! Now a trifle higher—so. And for the last, if Madame will permit . . ."

His hands flirted now beneath my breasts. They moved higher. A caressing movement caused my nipples to erect.

"Sir, is this necessary?"

"The buttons, Madame, they worry me a trifle. Were I to be allowed to unfasten them a little . . ."

"As you wish."

I could see all in the mirrors. His cheeks grew flushed as he unfastened my bodice. The orbs of my breasts rose defenceless to his hands. Standing behind me as he was I felt a distinct projection in his breeches. A trifle indelicately I moved my bottom against it.

"And now if Madame will please turn."

I did so. We stood literally face to face. My dress was now unfastened to my waist. The rosy buds of my nipples were as stiff as thorns.

"You beautiful girl! What a superb figure! What legs, what a bottom, you must have! Black will suit you best. One of the smallest and tightest of my creations—a lacy frill to hide your pretty navel, but no more than that below. You should not wear drawers, of course, with such a corset. The long black straps reaching down to your stocking tops will frame your treasures divinely."

"I do not wear drawers."

The words appeared to act upon him as an invitation. Gathering up my skirts so suddenly that I had no time to resist, he feasted his eyes upon all, right up to the junction of my thighs. A tremulous cry escaped me. Making as if to fall I seized his member which was all but starting out of his breeches.

"Ah sir, it is I perhaps who should measure you!"

His rude hands fondled the pert cheeks of my bottom, the skin glossy and warm to his fervent touch. I parted my thighs a little to steady myself. I felt in danger of falling. Of a sudden his hand cupped my mount. The moisture and the curls apparently delighted him. Our lips met.

"Measure it you shall, but in the proper place."

Before I knew it I was lifted and carried to the couch. I knew now why there was a single indentation in the velvet, halfway along the seat. Many a female bottom must have been laid there.

"Sir! my companion! she waits for me!"

"The measurement will take but a minute. What divine thighs! What coral lips between! Lay your legs well open!"

"Sir, you affront me!"

I lay back. My stockings tops, my thighs, my treasure pot, my uncovered breasts—all were in evidence. Kneeling over me between my legs he uncovered his member in a flash. Its size was impressive, its stiffness undoubted.

I moaned and tossed as befitted my apparent coyness. He descended upon me. The swollen nut brushed my curls. Retracting a little it brushed my clitoris. As if frettingly I tossed my hips and endeavoured to evade his kisses. His palms descended upon the tops of my thighs, laying them flat and drawing them wider apart.

"Now you may measure!"

"Ah! one inch! Two, three, four! Oh sir!"

Truly he was within me. I had counted well. The swollen

flesh of his tool throbbed in my being. Our tongues met in salute at the delicious sensation.

"Five inches! AH! six—nay, seven! OH! you are filling me! No more!"

"Work your bottom—dig your heels into the couch!"

A further invasion of his hefty plug. He was almost in me to the root. Our tongues threshed. I moaned my pleasure. With a final brief lunge he swung his balls against my bottom and gripped me tight.

"How many?"

"Nine! Ah sir, you are well furnished. Withdraw and let me test the length of it again!"

Moving with steady strokes he caused me exceeding pleasure. The old couch creaked as no doubt it had done many times before. Emma was all but forgotten in our transports. The oily lips of my slit gripped upon him greedily. I longed to feel his effusion but wished not to hasten it.

"What a perfect mount you are! How deliciously the curls of your pussy rub and tickle! Press your belly up to me tighter and coil your legs about my waist!"

"The things you would have me do! You must inject me quickly or my cousin may interrupt us. What would you do then—raise her skirts in turn?"

"My God, yes! How wonderful to have you both together. AH! you are coming—I can feel it! What liquid bliss—you are soaking my balls!"

My lips moaned beneath his. Dearly as I wished to express my most erotic thoughts I held myself in check. His cock sluiced me superbly. A gigantic quiver seized him. I tightened my stockinged legs about his waist. His balls made a loud smacking sound against my bottom. I was in ecstasy. My belly tingled with the oncoming of a further crisis. Even as he spilled the first jets of his sperm I anointed his indriving knob with my salty sprinkles. The couch was wet beneath me. His spermatic pulsings seemed endless.

Finally we sank down, my legs holding high around him. Panting softly we exchanged such kisses as do those who have enjoyed so sweet a climax.

"Sir, my companion."

The warning was enough, much as we would have preferred to remain bathed in our mingled essences. His doughty member withdrew, literally steaming. Small drops of sperm anointed my stocking tops. I rose and tidied myself quickly.

"You will return? In two weeks?"

"So long?" My tone was chiding but forgiving.

I departed quickly for fear that my passionate nature might wish to enjoy a reprise. Emma had finished her periodical and sat looking annoyed.

"Eveline, you took so long!"

"So many styles, Emma—but do not fear, I have chosen well for us both, one of each shade."

"Oh, but do you not think that black is so dull?"

"Not in the prettiest of their styles, Emma."

I forebore to tell her that drawers need not be worn with such enticing attire. The tightness of the corsets drew the waist in and so displayed the violin curve of the hips. Above the frilly top the breasts were left perfectly naked. At the bottom, the lace curved just below the navel, leaving a perfect vista below of the curl-fringed mount with the broad corset straps running down the fronts and sides of the thighs.

It occurred to me as we entered our carriage that Madame

Dalmaine's thigh-length boots would make an enticing complement to the little corsets.

Emma would never comprehend such sophisticated attire, but I certainly intended to divest her of her drawers if an occasion arose.

4

"WHAT do you make of Mary, then, John?"

"A lovely lass, Miss."

The fellow's face was quite florid. It was the first time for many a long week that he had enjoyed my presence privately. Cock Robin would have done little work in my absence, unless he had had one or other of the servants, or some street girl. I hoped he had not descended to that. I asked him openly.

"Oh no, Miss!"

There was such shock in his voice that I smiled. John wanted to be certain always that he had nice, clean girls, it appeared. And a young lady like myself, though he did not say it. The hump in his breeches did.

"Poor John, has Cock Robin been idle in his nest? Show it to me. I love to see it."

Standing before me as I sat by my window, he rapidly unfastened the flap of his red plush breeches. Sturdy as a carthorse he displayed it, the head as rubicund and swollen as I ever remembered it. A passion took me. Beckoning him forward more I bent my head and slid my lips around the purplish crest. He groaned. Slipping my hand within his attire I palmed his balls. They seemed heavier than ever. Glistening with my saliva his knob exposed itself again to the morning light.

"I am not in a mood for it now, John. Mary would love it, I am sure. Have you tried her yet?"

"No, Miss. She's skittish and shy. I tried a kiss or two and it were lovely. She has real velvet lips, like yours if I may make so bold. I felt her breasts and touched up her bottom a bit, but we had no privacy so I couldn't as get her skirts up."

"Shame, John. You would make a handsome pair. Have her sent up to me and perhaps we can do something about it. Would you like that?"

He nodded fervently and forced his stiff member back in his breeches. His disappointment was obvious that I had not invited its salute, but the promise of my words put a shine in his eyes.

"How shall I act, Miss? Shall I leave her alone here with you?"

"Exactly that. Give me some fifteen minutes with her, make sure the coast is clear and then return. Lock the door quietly as you come in. I will have her ready, I swear. Fear not if she struggles a little—it will be mere shyness. Have her lustily and she will enjoy it. After that the way will be clear for you."

He was gone. Emma had left with her father to ride in Hyde Park. Papa was elsewhere, I knew not where. John would ensure that there were no other interruptions.

A timid knock announced Mary. Sippett had produced a new outfit for her. She looked charming, pretty and fresh. I drew her to my bed so that we might converse. I reminded her of the awful fellow in the railway carriage. The episode had provided a bond between us, I said. I wanted to repay all her discretion in the matter.

"Miss, there is no need. I has the money still. I'm wondering what to spend it upon for best."

"Perhaps something you would like for a little cottage of your own, one day, Mary. I know one who would like to share such an abode with you."

"OH! Who, Miss?"

"John. The poor fellow has such desire for you I fear his breeches will burst if you do not accord him your favours. He is a splendid man, you know. Very reliable."

Her colour ran high at my words. Mary twisted her fingers about and stared at the floor. The proposal quite flustered and flattered her all at once.

"Has he kissed you? And felt you, Mary?"

"A bit. I didn't mind it, but in the servants' quarters there's always someone about and Sippett is so nosey."

"Exactly, and there are no beds large enough or comfortable enough up there for your pleasures. Imagine on this bed, Mary, would it not be nice?"

I passed my arm around her shoulders. She trembled like a bird. Fingering her skirt casually I drew it up to her stocking tops. Too bemused to resist she gazed at me with open mouth. Her thighs were plumpish, silky and warm. Casting up her skirt higher and drawing her down so that we lay on our sides, I uncovered her thatch. The curls were thick and brown.

"Would you like him to, Mary?"

"Oh, I dunno, Miss! Oh, MISS!"

Her further cry was occasioned by the sudden but quiet appearance of John who deftly fastened the door as I had bid him. His cock was in a rare state of anticipation, forming a veritable flagpole in his breeches.

"Lie still, Mary!"

I held her shoulders. She trembled, endeavoured to rise, and then sank back. Her eyes gazed wonderingly up at mine and then endeavoured to hide themselves as John uncovered his flaming member. Truly, I could have entertained it myself, but a new whim was upon me. I wanted to view, to witness—as Papa had done when he had had me mounted by more than one lusty fellow.

"Oh, what a size!"

Mary uttered a long wail that would have risen higher in tone had I not smothered her lips beneath mine. Truly her mouth was as desirable as John had said. I savoured its sweetness and the pulpiness of its interior as her top lip rolled back under the pressure of my own.

She kicked and would have threshed wildly had I not pinned her down while John's brawny hands held her legs well apart. For a moment I dared not raise my head to look, being occupied with keeping her down. Her hips wriggled madly. A shrill cry lost itself in the enclosing warmth of my mouth.

John was in.

Or at least his stout member was all of one third in her grotto as I loosed my hold in order to allow him to fall full upon her. No sight was ever prettier. Mary was the dove beneath the lion. Her mouth was open as if in a look of perpetual surprise.

"Ah! it's too big!"

I bent over her anew. My tongue coiled around her own.

"Slowly, John—enter it inch by inch."

Grunting his pleasure he obeyed. His breeches slithered ever further down, leaving to view his big buttocks and the glorious appendages beneath his cock. My excitement was intense, yet curiously I felt no immediate erotic desire myself. I slid off the bed. I gazed at them. Half crushed beneath him, Mary herself seemed more and more entranced at the rude slow entry of his piston. The lips of her slit formed themselves in a perfect mouth about the stem. I raised her legs—limp as they now were—and crossed them over the hips of John.

His shaft was buried deeper. No doubt he found her exquisitely tight. My eyes were everywhere. I drank in the lewdness of their posture. Exposed by the upward folding of her legs, Mary's bottomhole showed its rosy, crinkled appeal. I longed to finger it, but desisted. This, I thought, was so often how I looked—exposed and docile and yet with flames of desire within.

A gurgling cry sounded from Mary. No longer able to resist, John had lodged his Cock Robin full within her furry nest whose perimeter ringed his root and clung to it as a baby clings to a finger.

"Miss, oh! she's tight! what a glorious slit!"

"Have her John—she needs it. Thrust slow and deep. Bring your knob to the rim and push right in again."

I was beside myself with pleasure. Casting myself again upon Mary I renewed my kisses. This time she responded. Her breath panted in my mouth. Her tongue dared coil about my own.

"Oh! it's lovely!"

"And big as your Papa's," I whispered in her ear. John could not hear me. It should be my secret. The lickings of her tongue in my mouth became lecherous. John bucked his loins, treating her to a rare shafting. His prick in its emerging glistened with her juices.

I opened her dress. Between us we toyed with her bubbies. John sucked upon one nipple, I upon the other. They rose in hard peaks between our lips. Her joy was delirious. I knew her pleasure. There would be others. I was minded to entertain myself more often now like this. The gates of freedom were once more flung wide open.

"Faster, John! Let her feel it! Is it nice, Mary? Do you like it?"

"Oh, Miss, m'am, yes! He's got such a big one, like . . ."

"I know, Mary."

My lips silenced her quickly. In her arousal she had almost spilled our secret.

"Work your bottom now, Mary, for he is going to flood you."

"Oh! I want it! Make him spill his juice! AH! it's lovely!"

Her head hung back. I leaned up. She was a perfect picture of lustful pleasure, her eyelashes fluttering, a high flush of pleasure on her cheeks. I had judged well. The faint squelching of John's more vigourous thrusting sounded. His balls whacked against her bottom in their joy. His eyeballs bulged. He was well at the peak now. With a giant shudder he collapsed upon her and worked frenetically. Jumping up I took again my grandstand position, kneeling beside them. Hugging him closely with her crossed legs, Mary duly wriggled her bottom. Its rosy orifice opened and closed perpetually like a tiny mouth. She was coming, I could tell. Panting they absorbed each other's tongues. A fine froth appeared around the lips of her slit. The big vein in John's member throbbed, ejecting its juice. In but seconds it was as if she had been lathered with soap.

Heaving their last, they clung together. Ecstasy plainly showed on their faces. Thus I let them rest for a long moment. John's doughty tool would still be bubbling out its last strings of come, I knew. She would feel each one. Her pleasure would be doubled.

"Go to your quarters first, Mary, and tidy up. You shall have more of the same before long."

"Thank you, m'am."

Cap and hair awry, her skirt much creased, she departed. John lingered of a purpose, I knew, to allow me to view his cock which lolled now over his breeches. His nostrils flared as I lay back on my bed and cast up my skirts. Lewdly I offered him the view between my thighs.

"You shall be her stallion, John. Treat Mary well—she deserves it. I will let you have her again soon. How pretty to watch you both!"

Taunting him so, I covered myself. A myriad ideas were spilling about in my brain. Even though I might not achieve all, I would do so with the greater part of them.

"I'll do as you say, Miss—ever I will. And now if you wants a little pleasure . . ."

He grinned and dangled his prick. The wetness—his own and Mary's—upon it made me feel lewd, but I desisted. The change in me puzzled him, but that was all to the good.

"It shall be in service soon, John. There is yet another warm-bottomed maiden here who requires a good poke, though she does not know it. Perhaps I will appease you after that. We shall see. You must play your role well—that is all I ask of you."

The fellow's eyes grew large. I detailed my plan—or such of it as I had hastily thought out. It was crude, but with a little manipulation could become more devious.

"And there won't be no trouble or shouting about it, Miss?"

"You have my word on it. She is ripe for pillaging, John, and who knows, may give you equally as much pleasure as Mary. Think carefully that your every move must be as I say. I shall tell you more later."

"Yes, Miss."

"Go quickly, John, for my cousin will return soon."

I was correct in any event in my forecast. Ten minutes later I heard the horses enter the stable, and hurried down. Emma's cheeks were aglow with her ride. She looked quite fetching in her riding dress and three-cornered hat, though her expression had the faintly doltish and dull look that I had come to expect of her.

"You must bathe after your exercise. Would you like me to attend to you?"

"Oh, I think not, really."

She looked confused by my suggestion, yet must have undressed before many another young female before. I overrode her and led her upstairs. Sippett filled the bath at my call. Helping Emma to remove her clothes, I arrayed a robe about her. She had a pleasing figure, her breasts and bottom quite beautiful. Her skin was as smooth as milk.

"Eveline, there is no need!"

"Nonsense. Are you not our guest? I must look after you."

I led her from her room toward the bathroom. The tie of her robe having been left deliberately loose I fingered the waistband at the back so delicately that she did not feel the motion. Precisely at that moment John descended to our floor. Emma's robe flew open. She gave a little shriek and endeavoured to cover herself while I in my apparent solicitude only served to ensure that John had a full view of her naked charms.

"Oh my goodness, Emma, how naughty of you!"

Pretending shock, I bustled her into the bathroom. For a moment she appeared quite speechless.

"The horrid fellow, he stared at me!"

"Really, Emma, how you displayed yourself! The poor fellow will be quite beside HIMSELF. You are a perfect little beauty, you know."

"Ah, Eveline, I did not intend it! You surely could not think so!"

I arranged my features in an expression that implied neither belief nor disbelief. Assisting her into the bath I allowed my hand to linger for a moment under her bottom. She gave a slight twitch and a jerk. My fingertips had eased beneath her slit and then withdrawn so quickly that the gesture was seen as an accident.

"Such things happen, Emma, sometimes for the best, sometimes not. London is a very excitable place."

"Oh! what do you mean?"

I laughed. I bent over and kissed her mouth before she could say any more. Indeed I urged her not to. My ways were subtle. They implied that I knew more than I knew, and that Emma, too, did. How physically responsive she might be had already aroused my curiosity. In soaping her I teased her nipples wickedly. They rose splendidly.

"Is it nice? The water, I mean."

"Oh, yes! But, Eveline . . ."

"We shall not talk of it, my pet. We are both old enough to know certain things, are we not? John has been with us for years, of course. He is very strong and lusty, I believe. You will have put him in quite a lather, I'm sure."

I reached beneath her armpits and tickled her. She could not help but laugh.

"He will not tell anyone, d'you think?"

"Tell? Oh heavens no. He will guard such a glorious vision to himself. He will have fond dreams, I feel certain.

Can you blame him? You are truly lovely. Would that I have curves such as yours. Get out and let me dry you now."

She obeyed. Under the power of my flattery she was lost for words. The towel passed between her thighs. She blushed and would have started away. I bid her be still or the drying would take too long. Couched beneath the towel my forefinger moved persuasively around her slit the while that I also rubbed her bottom. Her knees trembled. A sigh escaped her. As if by chance my finger slipped out beyond the towel and tasted the moist lips of her quim. She started and clutched me. There was a glazed look in her eyes. Her nipples pointed on her snowy mounds. I dried her breasts delicately, passing my fingers persuasively over the tips while—as if to steady her—I cupped her bottom.

"Such beauty! You must be one of the loveliest girls in London now. I will toast your beauty—I do declare it. Put your gown on and I will bring champagne."

"Oh, Eveline, how silly you are!"

Clearly she had never been so flattered. I flattered MYSELF rather at the role I had played. The subtle titillations of my fingers had been prolonged rather more than I have described. I had tuned her like a fine violin. Her bottom wriggled pleasingly beneath her thin gown as I led her back to her room.

"Do not dress yet, for you will become overheated. I shall be but a moment."

The door closed. The corridor was empty save for John who appeared exactly as I wished.

"You are ready, John?"

"Never more, Miss. Cock Robin has really perked up. Suppose she makes a screaming of it?"

"Then I shall come in—but she will not. Her cunny is warm and moist and just ready for your plunger. Ram her quickly—embed it, and hold it in so she can feel its throbbing. Then give it to her. You needs must finish quickly."

I passed my hand around the big rod within his breeches. It was as stiff as if Mary had never entertained it. John was within in a flash. A screech sounded. It was quickly muffled. A threshing sound came to my ears. I leaned against the door and prayed that no one would ascend or descend. A sobbing, a moaning, and then a silence. The bed creaked from within. John's groans of pleasure sounded.

"AH!"

It was a cry from Emma that was neither one of dismay nor pleasure, but rather of surprise. John must have reamed her to the full. I would have given much to have been a fly upon the wall. Warm and soft as she was from the bath her secret pleasure must have been intense, much as she apparently wriggled in John's grasp, as I later learned. Slippery as a fish and yet yielding in great part to the piston of pleasure, she succeeded in moments in drawing forth his sperm.

I coughed. It was the signal to John to uncork himself. The fellow had never had a quicker bout. Even as I opened the door, pretending alarm, he rushed past me.

"John, what is happening!"

"I dares not tell you, Miss. Oh, what a temptress that one is!"

I entered and closed the door. Emma lay upon the bed in a seeming daze, her robe rucked about her waist. Seeing me she gave a start and turned her back on me. Sobs exploded from her throat.

"Oh, Emma! What have you done!"

"He m . . . m . . . made me! Oh, Eveline!"

I slithered upon the bed. I gathered her to me. Resisting, she kept her back to me, her face hid.

"You bad girl! Oh! but you are all wet! Did you let him!"

My fingers were sticky with John's sperm which was running even now down the insides of her thighs.

"Eveline—you will never believe me!"

I turned her at last and kissed her mouth. My hand fondled her bottom and sought the groove. She made little resistance as I caressed her. My fingers sought her cleft and cupped it. It throbbed like a small bird. She had come, I guessed, and was ready to do so again.

"No one shall know. I can scarce blame either of you, Emma."

"Oh, but . . ."

"Let me make you dry. How wet he has made you. Was it big?"

"AH, EVELINE! OOOH!"

The briefest flirtings of my fingertip about her clitoris and her legs straightened, her eyes rolling. I knew the signs. I captured her lax mouth as if comforting her. Our tongues licked together. Quivering, she released her spilling treasure on my palm in liquid drops and then lay inert.

I kissed her brow and soothed her hair. In a moment she clung to me, trembling in the aftermath. As one soothing a child I moved my fingers back and forth beneath her slit. The puffiness of the lips displayed her pleasure. I rolled her over onto her back. Her eyes were vacant—a look of stupidity in them.

"How wicked you make me feel!"

The words were mine. The thought, perhaps, was hers.

5

MARY knew nothing of John's adventure. I decided not to apprise her of it. Though he was fifteen years her senior, they made an excellent pair. I was fond of them.

After dinner that evening Emma retired to play the piano in the music room. She was clearly nervous and blushed openly at the sight of John when he served the wine. He for his part was sufficiently discreet to avoid her eyes.

My uncle contrived to sit next to me. Several times his hand passed across my thigh as if by chance beneath the tablecloth. I afforded him a faint smile each time he did so.

"Did you make purchases with your cousin today, Eveline?"

"Yes, Uncle. We ordered some fine boots and some delicate underclothing. Tomorrow we shall order gowns and dresses. We had an excellent day, did we not, Emma?"

"Oh yes."

A foolish smile crossed her features. Certain that my words had completely exonerated her she recovered her spirits sufficiently to partake of several glasses of wine. My uncle meanwhile had furtively discovered the breadth and tightness of my garters through my skirt. I excused myself as soon as it was possible to do so. On the first landing upstairs he accosted me.

"You will both look pretty indeed in your new finery—especially your underclothing."

"It is of the briefest nature—a new style of waist corset, quite small and pretty. I fear you are unlikely to see me in that, uncle."

There was no one about. His arm encompassed my waist.

"Would that I could. Your figure is splendid. Did you not order pretty drawers as well to go with your corsets?"

"The mode is not to wear them. The corsets are for private occasions, simply to pretty ourselves."

"Beneath your nightgowns and with your stockings on, perhaps?"

"Perhaps. You must think me very immodest to mention it."

"One should know all that a young lady wears, dear Niece."

His encompassing hand, slipping upwards, dared to fondle my breast. Attired as I was only in a close-fitting velvet gown, the nipple was distinctly felt against his finger. His face took on a puffy look.

"How I have longed to kiss you! My goodness, how you have grown!"

"For shame!" I murmured, for in so saying he had pressed me to the wall, slid his fingers down into my corsage and pressed his mouth upon my own. The satin skin of my breasts came immediately to his seeking touch. A penis of quite remarkable proportions erected itself beneath his breeches. I allowed my belly to move against it.

"You have such a big key in your pocket, Uncle."

"One for which I needs must find the proper hole, my love."

Our tongues touched. I allowed my lips to part as if in surprise. My knuckles brushed his member.

"Do you know where the hole is?"

"Yes, but it were best that I showed you in your boudoir, Eveline."

"Would it not be improper? I have no chaperone."

My objections were overcome by simple means of propelling me by my waist within. In another man it would have been gallantry. In my uncle it was boorishness. But a plan was forming in my mind. Unwittingly he had given me the opening. I intended to see it through.

A girlish cry escaped me. I was carried to my bed and laid there. In a trice my skirt was cast up. His eyes glowed at the treasures he revealed. Smothering me with kisses he endeavoured to part my thighs. I resisted. My resistance served only to whet his appetite the more. Falling to his knees he pressed his mouth upon my bared thighs. With a great pretence of modesty I made to cover my slit with the folds of my skirt. It was swept away. My thighs were moist with the lubrications of his mouth.

"Let me see it but a moment! Ah, what pretty, pouting lips, what curls!"

I uttered a shriek that I was careful enough to muffle with my hand.

"Ah, Uncle, you dare not put your key in there!"

He endeavoured to part my thighs wider, to kiss my lovemouth. I resisted. I kicked. I put up a fine display of modesty. He rose and came upon me. I applied my lips to his own and permitted him to suck my tongue. His member, imprisoned still within his breeches, thrummed against my legs.

"Hold it but for a moment!"

I pretended a helpless excitement. My hand was drawn down between us. Released, his penis stuck up like a huge cucumber in my palm. The thought of emptying its juice delighted me, but my plans then would have been put at hindrance. Finding my palm receptive he commenced to caress my vagina in a somewhat crude and unlearned manner.

"How big it is—how thick! OH! Emma was right!"

"Emma?"

His astonishment was profound. I accompanied my words by rubbing it gently. The veins pulsed. The knob was at least as big as John's. I passed my thumb about its velvety head. A groan escaped him. Our kisses ceased. My expression told of great dismay.

"Oh, how indiscreet I am! Only pretend that you did not hear me say that."

"What little devils you must both be! I had no idea! Come, let me slip it within!"

"NO! Oh, you dare not—I shall scream!"

"Kiss me and rub it then—only that."

"Very well, but you are very wicked. I did not suspect it of you."

The skillful movements of my fingers brought him almost too soon to the peak of ecstasy. He uncovered my breasts.

His lips lavished themselves upon the snowy orbs. He buried his mouth between the jellied delights. Had he made haste to mount me then I could not have resisted. The lips of my slit pouted for pleasure. Their oiliness exuded on his fingers.

I moaned fretfully, tossing my head from side to side, but ever keeping my thighs as close together as possible despite his efforts to insert his knee between them. I rubbed faster. The throbbing in his tool became profound.

"Of what did she speak? Tell me?"

I thrust my tongue in his mouth as if overcome by excitement. His thumb had by chance rather than design encountered my clitoris. I clipped my thighs together, imprisoning his hand, and squirmed my bottom. A delicious sensation overtook me.

"That you have a big thing in your breeches."

"AH! Oh God, rub faster! I am coming! Open your legs, I beseech you!"

My dalliances had not been for nothing. I knew precisely when to judge the moment. A mere second or two passed and then he began to erupt. The first fountain of warm thick gruel spurted over my fingers. I splayed my thighs. It was too late for him to sheathe it now within me. Shuddering with delight he rolled upon my belly. I worked it against his frothing tool, clamping his legs with my stockinged thighs so that in the electric thrills of bliss he could neither move up nor down. The jets from his knob flooded my curls.

"Ah, to do it in you!"

I did not answer, but made a mewing sound as if my pleasure were answering his.

"Do not tell Emma what I have said!"

"You devils! What delights! AH!"

He was almost fully spent. The amount of his sperm was

considerable. It flooded my belly with a thick film. I rocked and jerked, holding him until the last drop.

"What have you done to me? Oh, what wetness! Get off—I must dry myself, my stockings will be ruined, and my dress!"

"What matters? I shall buy you a dozen more!"

"You will have need to, you naughty man, if you do this to poor Eveline again. Please, you must go. It would be terrible if we were discovered now. I must change my clothes before the others see me! Oh, what a horrid thing to do! Does it always come out like that?"

My uncle grinned and rose. I appeared to have enacted my part well. He believed himself the initiator.

"Better that it had been in your hole and then not a drop would have been spilled. It is the true key to pleasure, Eveline."

I got up and lowered my dress. I was in a veritable bath of his sperm. His cock lolled thickly. I put my hand to my mouth and eyed it as if I had never seen one before.

"Oh! it has grown smaller! Is it always so?"

"For but a little while. Your charms would soon enflame it again. Come, finger it a little and you will see magic. It will grow once more in your sweet palm."

He made to seize my wrist but I withdrew. I bid him again to hasten unless we were discovered. With great reluctance he concealed it and fastened his breeches. At the door I gave him the tenderest of kisses.

"Shall we play our little game again, Eveline?"

"Perhaps. You have got me quite in a fluster with that big thing of yours. Surely it would not go right in us? I mean, in me."

"Every inch, my pet. Will you lock your door tonight?"

"I must. Papa often comes to test it lest vagabonds or burglars enter the house."

I gave him my most demure smile. Little could he have guessed the workings of my mind. I intended to enjoy his cock to the full, but in my own way. A final kiss, a tremulous touching of my tongue to his and he was gone. Papa engaged him immediately in a game of billiards downstairs. I hastened to join Emma who was quite alone. Bringing wine and glasses I encouraged her to make merry a little.

"What have you been doing?" she asked me curiously.

"I was conversing with your papa. He is a very affectionate man. My goodness, he insisted upon kissing me for looking after your needs today. He is very robust in his manner, is he not?"

"Yes, I suppose. Did he kiss you much, then?"

She gave a little toss of her head and looked a trifle put out.

"But twice, silly—like this."

I bent over her and planted my lips upon her own. Mischievously I allowed them to linger. She blushed and jerked her face away.

"Eveline, you are so impetuous!"

"And you. Did you not enjoy it today?"

She knew what I meant. My forwardness was such that I made it appear to be encouraged by her own.

At eleven I joined Papa in his room, having locked my own beforehand in case my uncle ventured the door. I wore an air of mingled concern and excitement. My plan was such that I intended not to involve John lest Papa take a turn against him.

Emma and I had foolishly, I said, taken a turn about the park on our own that day. We had been set upon by ruffians who had at first endeavoured to seize my purse. We had fled —Emma in one direction, I in the other. I had sought passers-by but there were none—only vagabonds who lay upon the grass and jeered at my calls for assistance. Neither was there a bobby to be found. Distraught, I had returned to the scene whence Emma had parted from me and found her lying upon the grass, her skirts quite up.

"She had been rudely assaulted, Papa—or so she avowed. There were distinct stains of sperm upon her stockings. Her bodice was open."

"Good heavens, Eveline! The fellows mounted her?"

"But one. The other, by her account, stood by, his member quivering with lust. But before he could take his turn there came an interruption and they fled."

"Poor Emma! Did she suffer much?"

"Not perhaps so much as I would have done, Papa. Indeed, she afterwards seemed rather more composed about the matter than I would have thought. It seems she has been a little deprived of such attentions of late."

"What a remarkable event! And yet she seemed so composed at dinner."

"She has learned to dissimulate well, Papa. The fellow had a doughty tool, it seems."

"At least the villains did not attempt my Eveline. You are certain that you were not assaulted?"

I sat upon his lap. His hand passed up beneath my skirts. I parted my thighs and returned his tender kisses. The gentle undulations of my bottom produced a fine effect in his breeches.

"Dearest Papa, I would have told you all. Eveline has only you in her thoughts. But do you not think Emma sly? Should she not be punished for it?"

His eyes gleamed. His finger sought my cleft and found my button. I breathed a sigh of pleasure and increased my movements. I had not been entirely unconscious of the occasional glances of desire he had cast upon my cousin.

"A light birching would do her no harm, Eveline? I am sure that Edward would give her as much if he knew."

"And even more perhaps. Oh, Papa, you must not overexcite me tonight for I am tired. Emma deserves a lesson, I am sure. I assisted her in her bath today. Her figure is quite exquisite—the roundest of bottoms. A little humiliation will prepare her for a stiff result, I feel certain."

My meaning did not escape him. He literally covered me with kisses. I intended, however, to keep him in fine fettle for his engagement with Emma. I rose and fondled his upstanding member.

"Dearest Papa, you must not overtire it. We shall be discreet, shall we not? In the morning I will apprise her that I felt guilty in your presence and that you forced a confession from me. She will have to choose, I will say, between yourself or her father. I shall swear to her that you have the lighter hand. Oh no, Papa!"

He raised my skirt higher. He would have had me then had I weakened.

"At eleven in the morning, Papa. I shall have her in my boudoir. You may surprise us there. You will make pretence of smacking me soundly first."

I expanded my plan. My ingenuity pleased me no less than it did Papa.

6

BY dint of persuading Emma that she must try on some of my dresses I gained her presence in my boudoir the next morning. Bubbling with pretended excitement, I spoke of what had passed between her and John. I chose a moment when we had both divested ourselves to our chemises and stockings.

"The rude fellow forced me."

"Sugar me if you did not entice him a little, did you not? What charms you offered to his view! Such temptations, my pet, your breasts, your thighs, your bottom and your sweet mouth offer."

Before she could speak I had cast her down half beneath me on the bed. The memory of my caresses in the bathroom had not entirely left her. The same look of foolishness entered her features that I was to learn betokened a sly form of surrender. My hand encountered the silky flesh of her thighs. I cast the hem of her chemise up.

"What a lovely white belly you have! What a plump treasure between your thighs! You little garden there needs much watering, does it not?"

"Oh, Eveline!"

She giggled foolishly. I began to caress her. The petals of her slit grew moist to my fingers. Our mouths met. I passed my hand full beneath her and felt the roundness of her bottom.

"Kiss me and hold me, Emma, for I have a terrible confession to make!"

She would have started up but I held her down. I allowed my voice to break a little while sauvely rubbing my stockinged knee against her vagina. Her face grew puffy, her eyes wide as she listened. I could not help but tell Papa, I explained. He had forced the issue from me. I sought her mouth, beseeching her kisses of forgiveness. Despite herself she could not help but keep her thighs open to the excited rubbing of my rounded knee.

It was at that moment that Papa chose to enter.

His face was stern. In his hand he held a short birch, at the sight of which—and the thought of her uncovered treasures—Emma uttered a wild shriek and rolled over from beneath me, hiding her face.

The posture was exactly as I had wanted. Papa had been well rehearsed. He had sought Emma first in her room, he said. Now he had come upon a scene of depravity no less than that which had evidently passed the day before. I assumed tears and pleadings. Emma concealed her burning face deeper in the pillow, her inviting buttocks well upturned for his attentions. Out of sight of her I laid myself over the arm of a chair and with the utmost timidity in my voice invited Papa not to spare either of us for our wickedness.

"You confess your sinfulness then, Eveline?"

"Yes, Papa."

I affected a short cry as his hand made noisy contact with the leather arm of the chair.

"You have seen what you told me you had seen yesterday? Even as I have now come upon you in the most libertine of embraces?"

"Papa! Oh, Papa, yes, but pray do not make me speak for dear Emma!"

I uttered further pretended cries as a loud swishing and smacking was heard. The birch made as fine a noise upon the leather as it would have done around my bottom. Then with an audible sound of satisfaction, Papa announced that I might leave and wait in Emma's room while he dealt with her in turn.

Sobbing in a manner that could not but deceive her, I threw on my robe while Papa approached the recumbent Emma whose bottom cheeks offered their perfect roundness to his view. The carpet being thick, I went and opened the door and closed it again as if announcing my departure. Then as silently as I had performed this little trick I returned to Papa's side. I risked all if Emma turned her face, but I knew well that she would not meet his eyes.

"You will remain exactly as you are, Emma."

Papa's voice was one of great solemnity. His hand wandered slowly, as if in prior inspection, over her bottom cheeks. Emma gave a start and then relaxed in a posture of helplessness. Papa's fingers assumed a distinctly cupping position beneath the bulging half-moons. Motioning me to move with him he took then her legs and moved her around so that her legs dangled over the edge of the bed.

"At the first stroke of the birch you will commence the confession of your sins to me. I shall not desist until I am satisfied that I have learned all. Is it understood?"

Emma's head moved in an indication of obedience. She was clearly too petrified to speak. Her very ears blushed as Lord L. raised her chemise higher in such wise as to uncover her bubbies. Retreating down again, his fingers once more brushed the bold satiny hillocks. Then without further warning the birch descended. Well-soaked as the twigs had been overnight, they caused no undue harshness but were as fine strands of leather.

Emma gave a little yelp, though not such a loud one as I had feared. It was evidently not the first time that the birch had kissed her bare bottom. The pink traces left by the twigs gave me a considerable satisfaction. I was forced to hold my breath for long periods lest my rising excitement betray my presence.

"Well, Emma?"

Papa's tone was stern. There came no reply, though I guessed that my cousin would not long sustain her silence. I was right. At the second swish of the birch, which descended with a moderation that would have scarce scared a cat, Emma gave a hissing gasp.

Her confused muttering of "Yes, yes," was not the satisfactory response we sought. In another second the birch descended more smartly, causing her hips to jerk in the most luring manner. It was indeed my own first sight of the effects of the birch. I found it not displeasing. It was a vista that must in thousands of errant young ladies have confronted as many disciplinary school mistresses, Mamas and Papas.

Emma's stockings glistened up her legs, her thighs

milkwhite above. In her posture her bottom cheeks thrust up provocatively. Beneath them a fringe of downy hairs and a peeping of lovelips were such as would have provoked many a cockstand.

Papa's distended weapon twitched in his breeches. Standing as close as I dared, I caused my fingertips to brush up and down the concealed column as a ludicrous squeal of pretended pain broke from Emma. Her burning face was hid now in her hands. It suited me admirably. The velvety cheeks of her bottom blushed pinkly.

"You played with his organ, Emma?"

"Yes." The whisper was hardly heard.

"Continue, Emma, continue!"

Lord L. cast down the birch and applied his palm to her bare posterior in a way which I thought to be relatively gentle but which, continuing rhythmically, caused Emma's bottom to gyrate rapidly. The plump cheeks quivered, closed and relaxed alternately. Their pinkness increased. The sight was delightful. Moving silently behind Papa I passed one arm about his waist and commenced to loosen the buttons against which his weapon pressed. In a moment the ruby head surmounting the thick column of manhood passed between my fingers and emerged in all its girth.

Emma's hysterical attempts to offer a facade of fear had reduced themselves to a quiet sobbing. Her hypocrisy —which I had never doubted for a moment—did not affect the blatant immodesty of her posture as she suffered Papa's hand. Her thighs appeared to open slightly, betraying more of the moist cleft beneath her burning bottom.

"OH! you hurt me, Uncle!"

Encouraged by my soothing hand, Papa ceased to smack her and insinuated his fingers just beneath the pouting lips.

"Did he not toy with you so, Emma?"

"Yes!"

Her shoulders hunched themselves protectively at the rude invasion of Papa's forefinger which had urged within her slit. I knelt and drew his breeches down, bringing my lips into contact with the rosy head of his throbbing prick which caused him to tremble and move his finger faster in such a way that the excitement evidently communicated itself to my cousin.

Despite her efforts to remain coy and hesitant, she could no longer still the awakening fire which the spanking of Papa's hand had further kindled. Her bottom rotated. I pressed Papa gently forward until the engorged head of his lance hovered stiffly but an inch or two from the delicious portals.

He withdrew his digit suddenly, leaving her like a fish out of water. I rose and stood perfectly still. In other circumstances she might have sensed my presence, but her senses were now aflame. A rippling tremor of her legs was visible as Papa bent over her. The fierce warm rod of his desire slid gently upwards in the groove of her bottom to rest in the indentation at the top of the valley. There was a muffled gasp from Emma which she did her best to conceal.

"And in your sinfulness, my Niece, you felt his wicked tool burning thus against your body?"

"AH! Oh, no . . . AAAH! Yes!"

"And you permitted it to enter, Emma? To enter the very lovelips which you had allowed him so lewdly to toy with?"

A sob which I doubted not was real broke from her as Papa's hands slid beneath her recumbent form to cup the full melons of her breasts.

"Caressing you thus, no doubt, did he not?"

"Oh, Uncle!"

"Was it not so, Emma?"

I could scarce wait for the amorous moment that was at hand. Prudence made me step back cautiously. Still suavely caressing the pendant globes of her bubbies which had now begun to swell in response, Papa drew back a little until the purplish head of his stiff tool brushed the lips of her slit. I toyed with myself, longing to be in her place and yet experiencing ineffable thrills in watching.

"Yes, yes—he put it in."

Emma's moan was a mingling of despair and sensuous surrender. Neither could wait any longer. With impudent desire her bottom pressed back a trifle. The bulbous nose entered the portals. The lips parted to receive it.

"Right in, Emma?"

"Yes! Ah yes, right in!"

The sound that emerged from my cousin's mouth was one of undiluted pleasure as Papa slid his hands beneath her belly and drew her bottom back firmly. His mouth opened, his nostrils flared. He was enjoying her in the very sight of me. Urging his loins forward he sheathed the entire length of his penis in her moist love purse. In but a moment he was in her to his balls which, dangling beneath, pressed to the lower curve of her bottom.

"Ah, Emma! How warm, how tight, my wanton niece!"

Emma's bottom began to move back and forth in rhythm with his thrusts. The movement, at first gentle, quickened. Papa bent over her, fully obscuring her vision. Doubtless her tongue was in his mouth since their lips remained glued together. His hands groped her everywhere. Her bottom writhed with mounting delight. A small sluicing sound was apparent as his cock entered and reentered her quim. Suddenly his mouth broke from hers. He rose up, his knees remaining slightly bent. Seizing her hips his loins flashed faster. She received him at full speed.

"Does it pleasure you, Emma?"

She was all but speechless. I knew her condition. There are moments when even the lewdest words poured into one's ear are scarcely heard. Her fingers gripped the bedcovers tightly. It was as if she could scarce contain her breath. Then a whispered assent was heard.

I hastened to the door. My fingers closed upon the handle and turned it with caution. It yielded. In a few moments Papa would no longer be able to control the onrush of the delirious moment. Even as I passed into the corridor and drew the door silently to I heard the panting gasps from both which signalled the approaching crises.

I made swiftly to Emma's room and tidied myself. Within a quarter of an hour I heard Papa come out of my boudoir and pass along the corridor. Moments later I was within my room again. Emma lay upon the bed in a posture of total immodesty. I approached her quietly. Her breathing was so soft that I thought her asleep. I slid upon the bed. Her eyes opened and widened like those of a startled deer.

"Oh, Eveline!"

I waited for nothing. Skirt raised to my hips I allowed her burning hip to press against my belly. I seized her chin and gazed into her eyes with a solicitation and tenderness that I know well how to assume. I passed my hand as if enquiringly about her face. She stared up at me in total bewilderment.

"Ah, Emma, my sweet, my love goddess!"

She could not have but felt the utterance to be sincere. Her lips parted in childish wonder. My tongue protruded between them. It encountered her own. Fresh as she was from a fiercer, more commanding embrace, the softness of my caresses calmed her. My fingers encountered deep warmth and a thick, creamy moisture between her thighs. They trembled slightly but remained lax and apart.

"Eveline! Oh, Eveline!"

Her arms cast around me and drew me closer. I took advantage of her posture and moved upon her. My fingers toyed with great tenderness over the love-bedewed lips that peeped from her dusky nest.

"Who could resist you, Emma? You are a true goddess of love—a wanton who has found her throne."

"You know?"

Her voice quavered. Her eyes searched mine with a wildness she could not conceal. I continued to stroke her cheek while bestowing little pecks upon her erstwhile prim mouth. My finger found her excited love button. I caressed it delicately.

"I made to return, Emma, lest Papa deal with you too severely. I would have offered myself in your place beneath the birch, I swear. I made to open the door. I peeped. And then—ah then, I saw!"

"Oh, Eveline! I did not mean to—I did not intend to!"

"So you ever say, little minx. Speak not. What was seen shall remain forever a secret between us. I have sinned again—however unwittingly—in coming upon you in a moment of divine ecstasy. Do you forgive me? Only say that you do."

A deeper flush had taken possession of her cheeks. Her heavy young bottom began to make small, hapless movements as I excited her clitoris. I closed her mouth with my own. I would not permit her to speak. The devil was in me. I affected a breathing sigh of pleasure and drew her limp hand over the satiny surfaces of my buttocks. My belly writhed upon her own.

Emma's deepening pleasure bubbled upon her breath. An interior excitement could not but have seized her at the thought of what I had witnessed. The realisation that I had apparently buried my sense of shock beneath a wonderment that she could so smoothly seduce her apparently outraged uncle comforted her. She relaxed in what she undoubtedly thought to be a dream.

"How divine you were, Emma!"

It pleased me to see the tendons straining in her neck, to feel the soft moist bliss of her love passage against my own. My mouth brushed wantonly around her nipples. Her fingers began to grope amorously beneath my bottom. I moved sensuously as if in anxious response to her seeking.

"Ah, that I dare tell you what I saw!"

I moved upon my hip beside her. My finger entered her sticky quim. It literally swam with his spendings. Emma's more hesitantly sought my nest. I whispered to her lewdly to insert it. The tip of her finger entered. I bit my lip. I implored more. I affected a certain delirium which, from the passion of her kisses and the more agile movement of her finger, excited her in equal measure.

"How delirious you have made me, Emma! Ah, how naughty, how divine of you to have induced Papa to possess you as he did! Forgive me, but I could not help but see. He had his cock full in you! How you wriggled!"

Emma was helpless now in her belief that my overwrought state was due to the manner in which she had submitted her charms to Lord L. and that I was totally carried away by the two exhibitions she had now given. No doubt she thought of herself as the conqueror of the entire household. Our mouths and tongues joined in that exquisite softness and knowingness that only women together possess. Her stiffened nipples stung against my own. I passed my hands down tightly under her swelling bottom, so causing the lips of her sex to rub against my own.

"Ah, Emma, did he spout in you?"

It was the moment for the question. I had judged it adroitly.

"Yes!"

Her confusion swam hot in my mouth. I passed my finger between the rich hillocks of her buttocks and teased the tight, puckered rose that she would yet surrender. I whispered as one possessed. I spoke as if in hushed admiration of her skills.

"Did your bottom feel nice? Did you want it?"

"Eveline! Ah, yes!"

My fingertip entered her rose. She was exquisitely tight and yet I felt the treacherous yielding. Her tongue swam in my mouth.

"Would you have liked Papa's prick so—in your bottom?"

"Yes! Ah yes!"

She scarce knew what she said. It did not matter. I had brought her to a point of lewdness from which she could never now retreat. An hour later we held hands like accomplices as we made our way to Oxford Street to choose some gowns. Emma became a little quiet in the process. I had expected more jolliness from her. Her wavering of moods annoyed me. I grew impatient and selected dresses of silk or velvet for us both, ensuring in all cases that they were closefitting.

Finally I chose some nightgowns. We would have identical ones, I said.

I had my reasons.

7

"**M**Y carriage, John!"

"Let me help you with your bag, Miss."

The carriage, having been quickly summoned from the stable, John assisted me within. The fellow was all solicitude.

"How goes it with Mary, John?"

I lowered my voice so that Jim, the driver, would not hear. John leaned towards me through the window. He had had a rare night of it, it seemed. He had risked going into Mary's room and given her a "right good one."

"She was docile as a lamb, Miss, and loved it."

"You must teach her to have it in her mouth, John, I am sure she will like that, too. Forward, Jim!"

I had left Emma behind. The encroachments of the house had begun to bore me. I sought adventure. As usual I went not unprepared. In my case was all that I needed. Within twenty minutes we had stopped at a small hotel close to Victoria Station. Jim looked bewildered as I descended. He had expected a grander place.

"Here, Miss? Shall I wait? 'Tis not always too good a neighbourhood."

"I shall be perfectly well, Jim. I have come to visit a poor friend. I shall make my way back later."

I entered the dowdy reception hall. The clerk was bemused at the appearance of someone as well-dressed as I. It mattered not. The room I was given was evidently their best. It was small and tasteless, but I intended not to stay too long within it. Scarce had the door closed than I stripped to my boots and stockings and drew out an old dress and bonnet that I had found long before in the attic. How they had got there did not matter. They were sufficiently shabby for my purpose.

The clerk, being engaged, did not see me go out, nor would have recognised me from the back. Down the long street I walked towards Pimlico. I needed the exercise. The late afternoon was warm. Houses alternated with small, poor shops. Women leaning in dark doorways disregarded me. From all appearances I was one of their kind. Several men stared at me. I ignored them just as I did one who drove a cart slowly past and stared into my face.

"What a lovely one! Cor, Miss, want a ride?"

I did indeed, but not of the sort he first intended. I knew not my way in this district and clutched my purse tightly. It was a ragged one. No one would expect to find more than a few pence in it. As I approached the Pimlico district, the houses became a little better. Steps had been cleaned and doorknockers polished. A carriage stood outside one, from which a man of about thirty-five descended. Paying the cabman, he stared at me and then walked quickly across my path.

"Pardon me, but you are exceedingly pretty. Allow me to introduce myself. I am Edwin Pickles, photographer."

"Indeed? And how would that interest me?"

I placed a nasal Cockney twang in my voice, but my vocabulary evidently puzzled him. He was of neat attire and wore a sporting jacket and modishly tight trousers with black silk bands running down the sides. His shirt was open. Like the corset designer, he wore a cravat.

"I seek models. You would make a perfect one. I would pay you, of course."

"Oh! ain't you a lark! Naked I suppose?"

"Would you like to talk about it? I pay a guinea for first poses—more later."

I sniffed. I was remembering the manners and speech of some of the maids we had had. To imitate them amused me.

"As you like."

We mounted the steps of the house. The hallway was clean within. I was led into a sitting room, as it is called in such dwellings. Scarce had I sat than a woman appeared. She was much of the man's age and had a slightly common but attractive face. He introduced her as his sister, Edwina. Her eyes cast up and down upon me.

"This one will do, yes. A pretty one."

I affected to look pleased, pretended a bit of sharpness and tried to bargain for thirty shillings, but they would not have it. A glass of cheap sherry apparently assuaged me. I was led up two flights to the studio which had a large roof light. Couches, armchairs, and drapes of various shades lay about. On the floor were cushions. A painted cloth backdrop showed a rural scene. There was even a Penny Farthing, propped in one corner. In the centre of the room stood a large brassbound camera of mahogany on a sturdy tripod. The back of it was covered with a black cloth. A big brass lens gleamed at the front.

"Take your clothes off and I will pose you."

I had little enough to take off. My dress followed my bonnet. I stood naked in my stockings and boots.

"What a beauty! I swear you are the loveliest girl I have had here!"

"Then you should pay me more, eh? How about it?"

He was close upon me. Poor girls did not struggle very much, I imagined, if there were money in the offing. He made bold to caress my naked bottom. I wriggled it a little and cast my eyes down.

"Will you pay me more if I do?"

His erection was evident already. He pressed it to me, raised my face and kissed me. His hand sought my breasts. It was two days since I had been mounted and I still had visions of Emma in her transports.

"Another guinea, by God, you shall have it!"

"Promise? You got to promise! Oh my gawd, what a whopper, what a big one!"

We were on the cushions. Their purpose was obviously twofold. A shaft of impressive size quivered in my grasp. His mouth smothered mine. I absorbed his tongue. Breeches sliding down, he prepared himself for the assault. I would have preferred some preliminaries, but my lust was as great as his. I panted. I guided the knob to the orifice. It sank within. A gasp of pleasure escaped us both.

"My, you're lovely! What breasts, what a bottom—it's as round as a peach! Put your legs up over mine!"

I obeyed. It would not do to be too forward with my skills. His cock sank in me to the root. I squeezed.

"Oh! you're hurting me with it! Don't go too fast!"

"There, there, you'll like it in a minute. Hold it in. Can you feel it throb? No one ever brought it up so quick, I swear. What a perfect fuck you are!"

"Suck my tits, then—I likes that."

He began to thresh. His piston moved in my spongy clasp. I closed my eyes and felt a complete delirium. There are occasions when I can be mounted three times in a day and then feel that the fourth is the first I have had for weeks. It was so now. I bucked my bottom to encourage him.

"Do it fast—I like it! Make me come!"

"You beauty! Oh, what heaven!"

His knob seemed to be thrusting up almost into my womb. His balls made a fine smacking sound. Beneath the cushions the floorboards squeaked. I was wet already with my spendings. The perfect, simple glory of the act overcame me. Those who scorn such "wanton pleasures" know nothing of the richness of experience such as only the truly initiated can enjoy. My pleasure was twice and thrice his own, had he but known it. Lithe in his movements he pumped it back and forth, his cock well oiled by my juices.

"Don't come in me! Suppose I 'as a child?"

Too far gone, he did not care. I pretended of a sudden the same abandon. I heaved to his heavings. Our pubic hairs rubbed together. My nipples were stark against his chest.

"You like it? Have I got a big one? Is it nice?"

"Oh, I loves it! Do it more!"

He shuddered. His words had been meant only as a prelude to his climax. Jets of warm come streamed from his prick and flooded me. The sensation was delicious. I alone, it seemed, could enjoy such pleasures and remain free of complications. I absorbed him like a sponge. He groaned in my velvety depths. Our bellies squirmed. Then he sank down. He panted mightily. We lay soaking until at last he decided to withdraw and rise. I rose and flopped into an armchair, feeling a little pool of sperm issue itself under me where it spilled from my cleft.

His eyes were somewhat rapturous as he covered himself and gazed at me. Indolently I let my thighs fall apart.

"You didn't 'arf fill me up, you did!"

"You'll come again tomorrow? I can photograph you then. The light isn't good now."

"Tomorrow? I ain't got nowheres to go tonight."

He looked bewildered. He ruffled his hair. His eyes could not take themselves from my muff.

"Very well. I will speak to my sister."

He was gone. I looked around, saw a bottle of wine that had been newly opened, sniffed it and drank a little. My throat was parched. I replaced the bottle hastily when he ascended again.

"There is a spare room. You may sleep there."

"You said as you would pay me two guineas, remember, and I 'as to get my supper."

"All right. See, I have a half a crown on me. Take that and we will settle in the morning."

I took it quickly and placed it in my purse where I had otherwise only placed notes so that they would not click together. He would think it otherwise empty. Having put my dress and bonnet back on I went down. His sister waited for me in the hall.

"I suppose he had you? He does that with half the girls. It's disgusting!"

"I don't know what you mean—I'm a decent girl, I am. Don't you go besmirching my name or I'll make ructions about it, that I will!"

I pride myself as an actress. She could not help but be convinced. I take care always with the expressions in my eyes as well as the words that come from my lips.

"Nothing intended. After you've got your supper you can come back. Second door on the left, first landing, is your room. Has he paid you?"

"No. I ain't done no posing yet, 'ave I?"

Perhaps she thought to catch me out. I gave her a stare and departed. I had no need to return. The thought that I had earned two shillings and sixpence by enjoying myself was extremely amusing. I had learned something at least about the economics of copulation among such people. Entering an eating house I had passed on the way I saw a young girl standing there. She had dirty golden hair, a ragged skirt, and worn-down shoes on. I imagined her sixteen or seventeen. Our eyes met.

"Got a penny to spare, Miss?"

"Are you hungry?"

"Yes, Miss. I ain't eaten only but a scrap of bread since morning."

"Come in with me. I will buy you something."

I was moved by her prettiness and her poverty. She could scarce believe it when I ordered mutton chops. The grease ran through her fingers. She was in heaven. I gathered she lived in Stepney. Her mother beat her and she had run away from home. There were thousands of such poor children homeless on the streets. Her name was Alice.

"Would you like to earn money, Alice?"

Her eyes were as big as saucers when I explained. No, she didn't mind taking her clothes off. Her brothers had seen her often enough like that, and her father. They all lived in one room. When her mother was asleep she had played with their "diddles," she said. They called it tickling. She liked being tickled. It was a rare lark, she said.

I took her back with me, her tummy full. Before leaving I got the man who owned the eating house to wrap some cold meat and pickles for us in a piece of paper. It would serve as our supper or breakfast. Alice danced along beside. I think she was sure I was a lady but would not dare say so.

Edwina received us at first haughtily but changed her mind when she had had a good look at Alice. In the sitting room she lifted the girl's dress and displayed a perfect, chubby bottom, handsome young legs and a fine down of curls.

"She'll do. Edwin can photograph you both together."

I guessed what that meant. We slept together in a narrow bed, huddling close. I gave her a little "tickle" before going to sleep. It made her feel nice, she said. My finger worked smoothly in her soft cleft. She hugged and kissed me, then straightened her legs and gave a sigh.

"Did you come?"

"Yes. I like that. Ain't it lovely?"

She would not confess to having had either her brothers' or her father's cock in her, but I guessed she had. She was a warm little thing, fully amorous when started up. Bread and drippings and a mug of tea sufficed for our breakfast. At nine Edwin began photographing us. We assumed various poses, but it was necessary to remain perfectly still for each one while Edwin counted solemnly. Little by little he encouraged us until Alice lay on her back with her legs in the air and I held my tongue close to her slit.

"I mean to have a young fellow to pose with you girls now. Would you like that?"

I said nothing. Alice stared and giggled. The young man was presented. He was scarce more than a year older than Alice. His eyes would have eaten me up. I wore black stockings and nothing else. Edwin had provided gaudy garters which clipped my thighs tightly. Undressing as if embarrassed, the newcomer, who was named Charlie, presented a slender figure to our view. His penis looked equally thin.

We took our first pose with Charlie between us, he kissing me and Alice holding his cock. In a trice it was up. Though of small girth it was of reasonable length. At Edwin's command I lay on my hip and took it in my mouth. The long seconds passed while Edwin counted. I sucked seductively upon the pear-shaped knob.

"Let him do it? Would you?"

"Half a crown extra for that if I do."

The photographer frowned. He regarded me obviously as a hard bargainer. By any working girl's standards I would be coming into riches.

"Very well. Kneel up. Have Alice lie under you. Keep your bottom up. I want you and she kissing while he holds it in."

I presented a bottom as perfect as any that Charlie or Edwin would ever be likely to see. A thought had seized me that I could not resist. Passing my hand under me I took Charlie's stiff little penis and guided it—not in my slit but against my rosehole. Whether he had ever entered it in a girl before I know not, but he made no ado about presenting it there. Edwin, busy with his focussing beneath the black cloth, was at the wrong angle to see what was happening. Charlie groaned. I do not blame him. I was still then a trifle tight there, yet he proved a perfect size to initiate me in this respect.

A sob of pleasure escaped my mouth as it settled upon Alice's. The minx, excited, thrust her tongue. I moved my bottom back carefully on the doughty little rod whose knob was already pressing beyond the puckered rim of my rosette.

"Be still!" Edwin commanded.

Charlie's hands clasped my hips. I dared not move. I wanted it too much. Fortunately at that moment Edwin fussed again beneath the cloth. He was forever rearranging his focussing and twisting the lens about. Quite beside himself meanwhile, Charlie inserted himself a further inch . . . another! Ah! the sensation was beyond description. My tongue twirled about Alice's. If I had measured the corset designer, then I measured Charlie's piston much more sensitively. I had reason too. There was a slight burning and itching, yet the pleasure was immeasurable. A sensation that the breath was being expelled from my body overtook me and then passed. I had absorbed five inches of his tool when Edwin again sternly bid us be still.

We froze our postures—externally at least. Within my bottom Charlie's prick pulsed its pleasure. A gurgling sound escaped him though he managed to keep perfectly still. Within seconds—the very sounds that Edwin was devoutly counting—I experienced the long shoots of Charlie's sperm that for a blissful moment seemed to throb endlessly and appeared to jet right up into my bowels.

The pleasure was rapturous. Too often in my delights I had failed to feel the spurting of the male liquid in my slit. Now in my narrower, tighter passage I could feel it all —ALL.

The photograph was taken. Charlie withdrew as slowly as he could. His sperm trickled warmly from my bottomhole. Falling back, he appeared to grow pale, his cock oozing. Edwin—not knowing exactly what had passed—thereupon berated him. The further poses which should have included Charlie's young manhood, were ruined, he said.

"I am tired anyway. You must have taken enough."

I made my tone clipped and certain. I rose to put on my dress. I wanted to absorb in my mind the experience I had received as much as I had done in my bold bottom.

"Is he going to pay us now, Evie?"

"Yes, he is. Are you not, Edwin?"

I had forgotten my Cockney accent for a moment. All

stared at me. A certain furtive look came into his eyes. Overtones of false geniality entered his voice

"No time to go to the bank today, you see. I tell you what—come back tomorrow morning and I'll have it ready."

"You must have some money. Ask your sister. Does she not keep your purse?"

"She is out." His face was sullen.

"Very well—we will return as you say."

Alice looked bewildered. I believe she thought that both the photographer and I had conspired to welsh on her. I gave him no more of my time and led her down.

"He ain't going to pay us, Miss, I knows it."

"Oh, he will pay us, Alice. You know I am not as you believed?"

"Oh yes, Miss—I guessed you was a lady. I knowed you was doing it for a lark, but now I ain't got a penny and nowheres to sleep or go."

I hailed a carriage. It was the first one that Alice had ever been in, she said. In a few minutes we were at the hotel. The clerk, perceiving my face and then my clothes, nearly fell off his stool.

"This young lady will stay the night here instead of myself. It is paid for and therefore it does not matter. See to it that she gets what she wants and I will reimburse you."

He nodded in a surly manner. I threw a note down before him. His expression changed. He stood up.

"Yes, Miss."

I changed again and settled Alice in, giving her the half crown that I had received from Edwin. She would be able to buy food a-plenty with it.

"You will come back, Evie?"

Her gaze was solemn and anxious. I assured her of my word. She was a charming little thing. Papa would appreciate her once she was bathed and cleanly clothed. I felt certain we could find a place in the household for her. She and Mary would get on no end.

I made my way down to the street. Cabs were a-plenty at that hour. One stopped expectantly beside me.

"Anywhere to go, Miss?"

"Yes. Scotland Yard, please."

8

"INSPECTOR Barkey is not here, Madam. Would you wish to see someone else? Can you tell me what the matter is about?"

The policeman who received me regarded me so closely that I imagined my dress had become transparent.

"It is a matter of some confidence. Who is the other senior officer?"

"Chief Inspector Ramage. I dunno whether he can see you now or not."

The matter, however, was swiftly arranged. The Chief Inspector was a man of some physique. He accommodated me in his office. His eyes scanned my figure with more than passing interest. I affected my quietest manner as one who is deeply shocked. I had chanced upon a young girl, I told him, who had fallen into the hands of pornographic photographers. Not only had they made devilish use of her, but had refused to pay her and thrown her out of the house into the bargain.

"The devils! There are a number of these people about now that photographic work has taken on. We shall have them, Madam—I swear on it. Can you explain the nature of the photographs to me?"

His gaze was somewhat expectant. As if summoning himself up for some ordeal he partook of a glass of whisky and offered me one. I sipped my own delicately.

"The photographs were of an extremely intimate nature. I do not know whether or not I dare speak of them to you. In one, for instance, the poor girl—quite naked save for stockings, was bent over a chair. . . . Oh! but I cannot describe it!"

His look was immediately solicitous. He rose and came round his desk.

"Do not fret yourself. I believe I know well what you mean. Allow me to show you. Perhaps if madam could stand a minute?"

I stood. My breasts made somewhat intimate contact with his chest. A slight hoarseness entered into his voice.

"I has to be certain, Madam, that the postures were within the meaning of the Act, if you catch my meaning. She was bent over, you say, right over, and all showing."

I lowered my gaze. My breasts rubbed across him.

"If I show you, will it clear the matter up for you?"

"Indeed it will. If you turn round now—so. Take no fright now for I am just going to bend you over and draw your skirt up a shade. You say she was naked?"

"Yes. You will have to arrange my skirt higher, I fear, to get the full effect. Oh dear! am I showing all now?"

"All that is perfect. And another scoundrel were right behind her, if my guess is right. Putting it up her?"

"AAAH! OOOOH! Is that your truncheon, Inspector?"

"Not the one I use on the villains, m'am. This one is to pleasure the ladies. Still now—jut your bottom up a bit. Ah, what lecherous likenesses they must be indeed, yet none would show as pretty an offering as yours. Steady now and we will get the posture perfect. Like so, was it?"

"In . . . In . . . In . . . Inspector, AAAH! Oh my goodness, it is in! You are stretching me! No more, oh I beg you!"

"We'll never know otherwise, m'am. Legs apart was it?"

"Yes! A bit more! Be careful of my stockings! Oh, you rogue, you are slipping more of it in. It's too big! Ah, what a thrust! Oh goodness, what a feeling it is!"

"Straddle your legs—keep your ankles firm. Another couple of inches does it. There—steady now—bend a little more. I love a girl who offers it up like this. Younger than you, is she?"

His cock was superb—a genuine ramrod of stiff flesh and muscle. With the last effort of his forcing it all in I felt his balls swing under me. A final squelch and nine inches of his weapon were within. I all but fainted with the delicious sensation.

"Ah, you naughty man, you are making me do it! Do you like my cunt? Is it tight and soft for you? Unbutton my dress —caress my breasts! OH! Yes! AH! Pump me hard!"

Our pretence had ceased. We were in the full throes of it. The buttons of my corsage flew apart. His big palms cradled the gourds of my tits. Bent over well as I was, it is a posture I adore. All propriety left me. I moaned and twisted. My bottom rotated lewdly against his belly. The warm silky orb enraged his lust further. His strokes, powerful and deep, quickened.

"Give it to me! Push it in! Oh, what a monster you have! Do you get many young ladies to do this to?"

"None as you. The working class lassies is easy. Many a one I've had in a dark passageway if she were afeared I were going to arrest her. Little devil! You know how to work your bottom, don't you?"

I was beyond reply. The friction of his big thick cock had already made me spill my libation twice. I was on the brink of another. The room seemed to swim about me. His loins were lusty. I suspected he could run a second bout in as quick a time as any man. And so it proved. Having inundated me, he uncorked and sat me upon his lap.

"Was it true, your story?"

"Of course! I will lead you to the young girl herself—and then to the den of vice. Promise me only one thing. The latest photographs taken must be destroyed. I do not wish them to appear before the courts."

"I shall find no trouble in doing that. Move your bottom on my cock a little. I never knew a girl to stir me so!"

My nipples attracted his lips. He sucked them greedily. His hair was thick and dark. I stroked it encouragingly while he was about his task. Beneath me the thick worm stirred and transmuted itself into a small pole that almost lifted me off his lap. I groped and felt the girth of it, slimy with love's spendings.

"Do you want to again?"

"Clear your desk. I will lie on it with my legs hanging over the edge. It will be nice that way. Do not soil my dress. Oh, you rogue!"

He was upon me again in the minute. A second bout is often the best. They take longer about it. Their cocks are less feverish, but even more willing. We panted, kissed and murmured our delights. After three or four minutes he inundated me anew. My thighs were wet with his come. I wiped them as best as I could with my kerchief while he watched and grinned. I truly believe he expected me to stay long enough for a third injection.

"What a lot you do in me!"

I could not help but smile. His pride was obvious.

"And shall do again, m'am, if the pleasure takes you. As to the whereabouts of these rogues, now."

"I would like to accompany you, Inspector. I wish to assure myself that the photographs of Alice—the girl I spoke of—are truly destroyed. Unfortunately at the moment I have another engagement. Can you not secure the villains tomorrow?"

"As you wish. A few more hours will make no difference. And the young girl concerned? I have to take her statement down, you understand."

I hesitated, but it would do no harm for Alice to have a little company. He would take more than her statement down, I felt sure. I gave him the name of a hotel. His eyebrows raised. I hastened to explain that I had paid for her accommodation as an act of mercy.

"You are a good 'un, all right, m'am."

"I try to be, Inspector."

He would not leave for an hour or two, I guessed. I hastened back to Alice who sat looking rather forlorn. I apprised her of events. Her first thought was of her money. I opened my purse and gave her a guinea. She clutched it as though it were the last coin in the world.

"The Inspector will call soon to see you, Alice. You will tell him everything and show him what you did. You won't be shy?"

"Oh no—I like a bit of company. When shall you come back?"

"In the morning."

Emma was of dull countenance again when I arrived back. She had missed me, I believe. Papa, passing us in the corridor shortly after my arrival, greeted and kissed us fondly in turn. My cousin tensed slightly as he did so. A frown crossed his well-cut features. I made an excuse to Emma upon some household matter and went after him. I drew him into the music room and immediately expressed my doubts about her.

"I am concerned, Papa. She does not appear in a mood to invite you to bed again."

"I agree, Eveline. The matter could become serious. Suppose, if she has doubts, that she decides to speak, to make certain matters known?"

I am too quick-witted to be put out by such a situation, especially when its source is one for whom I have no genuine admiration. Cousin Emma's behaviour presented a complication at once needless and boring. I doubted that she would so easily accept another chastisement, or that it would do any good. I decided quickly upon a plan which I communicated to Papa. His pleasure at my ingenuity was extreme.

"It can scarcely fail to work, my love, given your persuasive powers."

"It shall work, Papa. Your Eveline has your concern at heart."

It was a plan of some ingenuity, its only frail link being that its success rested upon the co-operation of the very one whom it was intended to ensnare and silence: my cousin. I instructed Papa fully. I knew he would not fail me. It was fortunate, moreover, that my uncle was away for the single, critical period that I needed. Had he been about the house in these few hours I might not have been able to engage Emma's attention as I needed to.

It may seem strange that I should distance myself from her to do so, but of intent I retired to my room instead of going to hers, as I had promised.

I had but only fifteen minutes to wait within before she appeared. To her unsubtle eyes I looked disconsolate.

"Something is troubling you, Eveline? I waited in my room for you."

My soulfulness would have convinced a saint. I beckoned her dully to sit beside me on the bed. I laid my hand casually on her thigh.

"Dare I tell you, Emma? Will you upbraid me? It is Papa. . . ."

"Your father, Eveline?"

She had the grace to blush. Her feet moved uneasily.

"Oh, Emma, you do not comprehend! The moment of splendour that you accorded him so sweetly—it has left him forlorn."

At this she made to interrupt me. The flush in her features appeared to stem from annoyance. I went on quickly.

"He will not speak of it, and most naturally he could not speak of such a thing to me. Yet I cannot but sense a feeling of desertion in his soul lest he cannot just once more taste the blissful embraces of his adored Emma."

"Oh, Eveline!"

The idiot appeared as if shocked. There are such women. They will take a man to bed one day with a great sense of passion, and the very next will act towards him as if he were a total stranger. It is as if a vacuum existed within them. When I myself have acted so, it has been for different motives.

"Dear Emma . . ."

I kissed the corner of her mouth softly.

"Dear Emma, I am truly aware that your exquisite favours are not granted lightly, yet you were so patently rapturous in Papa's arms. . . ."

I deliberately left the sentence unfinished. My large eyes shone full of hope and appeal. I dared all. I fell to my knees before her, as if in supplication, and passed my hands up beneath her skirt, laying them upon her rounded knees.

"Whatever passed between your father and I, Eveline . . ."

"Was incomparable," I interrupted earnestly. Moving with stealth and yet with the same seeming appeal as I looked up at her, I spread my fingers about the warmth of her thighs. "You know it was," I simpered.

"Oh, Eveline!"

A slight and apparently careless pressure of my hands made her topple back, though I suspect that it was to hide her confusion that she did so. I rose as if excited, my hands following the movement until she was bared to her thighs. She began to giggle. It was a stupid sound. I cast myself down beside her. A smile of radiant hope illumined my face.

"Say only that you will, Emma!"

I encompassed her lips with mine. They yielded. To my astonishment the mask of pretence had already begun to drop. The volcano had begun to simmer.

"Eveline, how wicked you are."

Her voice was one of wonderment.

"I, Emma? It is you—can you not see it? There are moments when I believe you truly fail to know the exquisite pleasures of your embrace. Can you imagine for a moment that I could have witnessed Papa in such a shocking state of Nature with you—responding to you afterwards as I did—if you did not breathe the very air of love, of passion, of desire? You have revolutionised my thoughts if only you but knew it!"

"Ah—I cannot—I dare not—not again!"

The token pretence fell from her lips with all the hypocrisy of a Sunday preacher. She waited, as I well knew, for my denial. I gave it with my lips on hers, as if in passion beyond control. She succumbed. Our tongues licked. My fingers sought the haven of her nest. They entwined themselves in the curls. They stroked the lips. Emma sighed audibly, her arms now tight around my neck.

"But once before you leave, dear Cousin, for the sake of dear Papa."

Before she could utter another refusal or pretend one, I slithered to my knees and pressed my lips upon her warm, moist slit. My tongue merged and licked exactly as I had learned from Madame Dalmaine. The effect was electric. Her moans sounded, her hips bucked. I lapped unceasing, I held her thighs. The tremors in her body became violent. A moment or two later the salty sweetness of her effusion sprinkled my lips. She lay inert, eyelashes fluttering. I moved up beside her again.

"You will, Emma? Papa goes to his club soon. He returns close to midnight. You have but to slip into his room a little before that. Meanwhile we shall spend delicious hours together."

"Yes."

The word was but a sigh, yet it came. I began to disrobe her completely. Within an hour we had exhausted one another so completely that we slept like angels. Awaking first, I locked the door and hastened to Papa's room. I acquainted him with the results of my experiment.

"She will accede, Eveline? You are sure?"

"Have no fear on it, Papa. A slight dosage in her wine at dinner will soften her further. I shall accompany her to her room. Within half an hour she will be ready to accept man or devil."

We hugged one another in glee. His reward would come simultaneously with Emma's—though she knew not yet the real nature of hers. I aroused her and persuaded her to bathe and perfume herself for the coming bout. Papa absented himself from dinner. It was thought best. I had arrayed my cousin in one of my lowcut gowns. At table my uncle appeared as much entranced by the sight of her half-uncovered breasts as my own. Several times, I swear, when he had one hand on my thigh beneath the tablecloth, his other was on her own. Her shiftings about became apparent. Finally she excused herself.

The door closed. The servings were completed. We were alone. Without ado my uncle rose, bent over my chair and placed his lips fervently upon the half-moons of my breasts.

"Ah, that I might fondle them properly tonight!"

"Oh, Uncle, there would be a scandal. I fear lest Emma might discover us. She is a little jealous, you know. I told her you had kissed me—in affection only. She was quite put out."

The words merely increased his excitement. He drew me up. The chair scraped back. In turning to avoid its arms I fell against him. His erection made itself throbbingly known against me.

"No one shall know, Eveline, I swear!"

"Such wickedness! Do we dare? At least Papa will not return tonight. I intended in fact to take his room—his bed is the most comfortable. Ah, but if you disturb me I shall struggle!"

He laughed. He read assent in my eyes. My fingers trailed across his rampant cock. The enormous knob pressed within the cloth.

"Struggle then, my sweet, for it will be even more delicious."

"I expect so!"

I fled as if in confusion. A generosity of port wine had done its work well on Emma. I undressed her in my room as one might a doll. Her breasts, thighs and bottom seemed to gleam with waiting ripeness as I held her limp and naked. I undressed in turn. We lay quiet, breathing softly, exchanging small secretive kisses. Several times I brought her almost to the brink of a bubbling climax, but would not assuage her completely despite her urgings. The supreme delight awaited her in Papa's room, I whispered. She hid her face hotly into my shoulder. We imbibed liqueurs.

My little clock ticked away the hours of her fate. I drew her up at last from the bed, having quickly established the deserted state of the corridors. In a moment I led her naked, glowing with love's fires, to the darkened bedroom opposite. The door opened silently. Papa had oiled the hinges before his departure. I urged her within, giving a final squeeze of encouragement to her warm bottom. As she moved—somewhat in a daze no doubt—towards the double bed, I closed the door in such a manner that she would think me gone. The corner of a broad wardrobe hid me effectively. In but a second or two my eyes grew more accustomed to the dim light.

Emma reached the edge of the bed. Her hands groped, her breath drawing in audibly with all the expectation of her aroused state. A small gasp escaped her as two brawny arms reached up, clasped her about her waist and drew her down.

Her face pressed burningly into his shoulder, Emma allowed her fingers to be guided to the stout penis that waited in full erection for her coming. His hand slid down the ivory smoothness of her back to palm and fondle her over-proud buttocks. Their mouths sought each other's blindly as his finger quested in the tight deep groove that separated the cheeks.

Emma sighed deeply into his mouth. Her prudishness seemed all but to have vanished. Relinquishing his waving cock she sought and weighed the heavy balls before gliding her hand up anew to tease the throbbing monster.

It was delicious to watch. His hand slid deeper under her bottom which—with the fingering of her slit—began to agitate itself wildly. Faster now her fingers slid up and down his prick until the moment could clearly no longer be delayed.

With a groan of satisfaction he swung her nubile body beneath his. Her thighs floundered eagerly, parting to receive him. The swollen nut of his distended prick passed between the succulent and well-prepared lips of her slit. As it did so he raised himself for the full thrust that would impel the thick truncheon of flesh full within her. It was in that moment that Emma's own vision seemed to clear. I sensed the opening of her eyes in wild disbelief.

"Papa!"

"Emma!"

It was a wondrous moment. He appeared to hesitate. Emma's legs flailed wildly, but she was already securely pinned.

"Ah! Papa, no!"

"On, my sweet! What rapture!"

A joyous groan and he was deep within. Emma received every inch. Her fingers clawed at his back in a seeming effort to save herself. Her face twisted from side to side. She attempted to cry out and succeeded in uttering only a low moan. Majestically his loins lifted and fell. The piston of desire began to stir and move within her. Her sobs filled the room.

"Oh! Oh, Papa!"

She could pronounce no more as his penis continued its long, persuasive strokes. Perhaps the thought came to her then—if she were capable of thinking then—that she would never dare confess the true reason why she had sought Papa's bed. Thereupon her face ceased to twist away. He grunted something in her ear I could not catch. Her reply was equally incoherent.

Their mouths glued together. The bedsprings sang softly. The pale orb of her bottom wriggled sleekly on his cupping palms. A tremor of delight seized both. Emma's legs rose and knotted themselves about his hips. The bedclothes twisted down. The conjunction of their parts was clearly visible. They were lost to all but the ecstasy of their pleasures.

I waited no longer. They were beyond hearing my exit. I hastened to my own room. Papa awaited me expectantly. I was in a rare froth of excitement.

"Emma?" he asked.

I slid into the bed beside him.

"She is conversing, I believe, with her Papa."

9

I DESIRED not to encounter Emma too soon after the events of the night and left early the next morning in company with Papa who went immediately to the Army & Navy Club. Emma would not think to ask about his presence and neither would my uncle. The fact that they had spent the night in his room would be sufficient to make them believe in his absence.

I repaired immediately to the hotel where I had left Alice. There—not unexpectedly—I found her abed with the Inspector. Or rather he in his shirttails was sitting on the bed quaffing coffee while Alice lolled beside him like the princess she undoubtedly felt.

She grinned but showed little dismay at my entrance. The Inspector's doughty tool lolled rather limply. It had done much inspecting evidently. His pleasure at seeing me again at such an early hour was exceeding. With pleasing tact, however, he did not attempt to embrace me.

"What's afoot, Inspector? Do you intend to catch the rogues today?"

"No doubt on it, m'am. I has six stout officers at the ready to pounce, and a cart to take away the photographic plates. They will be needed in evidence, of course."

"Of course—save those of this dear child. It would be a terrible thing if they came to light. May I propose a plan to you?"

"As you wish, so long as it don't impede our entry today."

"No, it will not do that. In fact it will aid it. I intend to visit there. I shall take care to leave the door unlocked. That way your men may enter quietly and take them by surprise. Meanwhile I will ensure that Mr. and Miss Pickles are caught in an unguarded moment."

He gazed at me with admiration. So much did it show that his penis began to thicken. Its bulbous nose peeped from beneath his shirtfront.

"You've given thought to this matter, I can see that, m'am."

"I do to all things, Inspector. It is now but nine A.M. Allow me until eleven. All shall be ready then. Come, Alice, get dressed and we shall depart."

"Yes, Miss. Will I gets my money?"

"Of course."

The little wanton was quite naked. Getting off the bed she drew out the chamber pot from beneath it, squatted, and piddled loudly. She being then out of sight of us, I passed my hand beneath the Inspector's shirttail and held his penis for a moment in my gloved hand.

"You have been most accommodating, Inspector."

"You, too, m'am. Perhaps we shall co-operate again."

His penis stirred. It began to assume alarming proportions. The tousled state of the bed afforded me lewd ideas, but I knew better than to succumb to them then. I gave his weapon a last squeeze.

"It will not be forgotten."

"Nor yours, m'am. We fitted 'em together nicely."

Alice was up and wiping herself with a corner of the sheet. I had stepped away from the Inspector. She had not seen my movements. His risen baton appeared as a tribute to her charms. In a moment her clothes were on. Bustling her to the door I looked back at the policeman who lay extended on the bed, his cock upthrust. It was a farmyard invitation. I smiled and shook my head. A quick breakfast at the eating house where I had previously taken Alice and we were ready for the fray. I told her all that I intended. Her eyes were aglow with complicity and excitement.

"We have come to photograph again, if you want us."

Edwina Pickles, who opened the door, looked more disappointed than pleased at our return. We were ushered in. Edwin appeared, looking rather pale.

"I had not expected you yet."

"It does not matter. The light is good, is it not? If you promise to give us some likenesses of ourselves we will do this one free. But you must pay us for the others that we done."

My speech was still an amusing mixture of cultivation and Cockney, but it did not matter. He appeared bemused at the invitation.

"Very well, then, but the young man is not here."

"We will pose together, Alice and I. You will have plenty of sale for such pictures. I know a few people who would buy them—well-to-do ones."

Their interest was immediately captured. The mystery of my identity added salt to the offer. Edwina accompanied us up to the studio.

"You are not a common girl, are you? Who are these friends you know?"

"Better to ask no questions, Miss Pickles. I am told they sell for two or three guineas a set—a fortune to some, a small amount to others. There are thirty or more men who would give a lot to see me naked in such pictures. First, though, you must pay us."

The money came immediately to hand. Edwina could not contain herself for curiosity. The idea of quickly selling thirty sets was obviously uppermost in her mind.

"Who are you really? Are you making a market of us?"

"Shall we have wine first? Let me pour it. I find it quite amusing to serve people instead of constantly being waited on."

There was no disguising my tone or manner now. I had them entranced. I expounded my themes. I was a high-born young lady of the best Society, I told them. The escapade amused me. I knew other young ladies of rank who would be equally daring, given the chance. Alice remained dumb with wonder. I satisfied them entirely as to my credentials without giving away a single name. While talking I refilled our glasses and passed into those of Edwin and his sister a few drops from a small phial that I had in my reticule. Papa had brought it back from India with him. I knew its power.

I continued my lecture, amusing myself no end. I reclined upon the floor cushions, so bringing them to follow suit. I had no doubts about the many poor girls they had cheated as they would have done Alice and I.

In a moment Edwina's features grew somewhat flushed, as did her brother's. Forewarned as she had been, Alice affected not to notice. The eyes of the pair assumed a glazed look. Their glasses lolled in their fingers. In a moment both sank back inert.

"Quickly, Alice!"

Edwina appeared conscious but incapable of resistance. We stripped her to her stockings. Her figure was firm and full. Arranging her neatly on her back, we spread her legs. Edwin was next. He attempted a faint resistance but was beyond strength to effect it. A slight dosage of an aphrodisiac in the drug had made his penis distend to a fine length and girth.

Edwina—unable to move—uttered a strangled moan as we rolled him upon her. Excited herself by the effects of the potion, the lips of her vagina were puffy and moist. To a hollow groan from Edwin his stiff weapon was neatly inserted. The knob disappeared slowly and was engulfed. Their loins stirred restlessly as if each were in a dream. Fetching some rope which I had spied earlier I bound him tightly upon her beneath their arms, rolling Edwina about until he was couched upon her again. Raising her legs, I brought them to his hips and—with the help of Alice —bound her ankles in such wise that her legs could not slide down.

I rose and gazed upon the spectacle. Had I known how to effect a photograph I might have taken a fine one then.

"Shall we leave them like this, Miss?"

"Look for the plates he took of us, Alice. They will be in those metal slides, I suspect, in the corner."

A neat pile stood there. Undoubtedly they were the ones. Edwin had not developed them yet. Removing them from the slides we shattered each one into several pieces. The evidence that most concerned us was now destroyed.

I gazed at my watch. There were yet six or seven minutes to go before the Inspector and his men arrived. I hastened down and unlocked the door. A carriage passing outside halted at my wave.

"Wait, cabbie."

I returned to the studio upstairs. Unable to resist temptation, Edwin had begun to agitate his loins. With her legs bound up about him, Edwina was in no position to say no. Her bottom began to bump merrily on the cushions.

"Quickly, Alice!"

We had just time to effect our escape before the policemen arrived. Inspector Barkey approached with his contingent. I waved and pointed to the front door which hung open. His expression was one of dismay that I was departing.

Emma was leaving the dining room as we arrived. Her face showed signs of dissipation as if she had slept little. Her surprise at seeing me enter the house at such an hour was great, but mingled with relief that I had possibly spent the night away.

"Sippett—this is Alice, a new girl. Take her in charge. Obtain a uniform for her. Tell cook she will help in the kitchen and otherwise. She will see Lord L. later as to her wages."

"Yes, m'am."

Sippett's eyes were all curiosity. I swept her away with a look and affected great pleasure in seeing Emma.

"I was called out last night. A friend of Mama's was taken ill."

"You have not slept much then, Eveline."

"Nor you, Cousin. You look pale. A glass of port will refreshen you best."

I guided her to the morning room. There, somewhat to

her trepidation, my uncle sat. He rose and greeted me formally. His eyes looked haggard.

"You had a good night, Uncle?"

"Splendid, Eveline—the bed was perfectly soft."

"But firm also, I believe. And you, Emma? Did you not rest much?"

"Oh! I am splendid, yes. Papa, are we not going to depart, today?"

"Nonsense, Emma, but you cannot. We have to try on the corsets and other things first. Your dear mama will be most displeased if I return you to Herefordshire without the town attire of a young lady. Is that not so, Uncle?"

"Truly, Eveline. We must pass a few days more here yet."

Emma, as usual, appeared put out. Nothing would finally do for her except perhaps a real birching. I displayed nothing of my thoughts, however. My manner was ever cool and sweet. I seated myself and poured port for the three of us without summoning John. Emma sipped hers reluctantly. Had I had my way I would have held her nose and poured it down. The more her dullness showed the more intent I became in completing her conversion.

"There is a ball tonight at the Claremont Rooms. Shall we not go, Emma? Papa will escort you and yours shall escort me—but they must not hinder us from dancing with handsome young men!"

It caused her at least to smile. My uncle gazed upon me hungrily, but I had determined not to assuage him yet. I had become vastly diverted by my subtle exercises of power. A richness of excitement arose again within me. I had yet to attain my twenty-first birthday and the accomplishments I had known were as nothing to those I now intended.

"You will excuse me? I have an appointment."

I swept from the room before either could reply. Before

closing the door I heard a shifting of chairs, a short muffled squeal from Emma, and then silence.

John approached.

"Shall I see to the morning room now, Miss?"

"No, John, it is occupied. Return within half an hour."

"Alice is a pretty little one, Miss."

I gazed at the fellow pertly. There were occasions when he was exceeding his station.

"No doubt, but you are not to interfere with her—I will not have it."

"Of course, Miss, it was but a passing remark."

I left him standing. His face was the colour of beetroot.

10

"ARE my boots ready?"

"Mademoiselle, such a *plaisir*! Please come in! Of course, I have been preparing them especially. Is the other young lady not with you?"

"She will come later, perhaps. Is your wife in? I would like to see her."

I was led into the *atelier*. There Madame Dalmaine greeted me with pleasure brimming in her eyes.

"Fetch the boots, Pierre."

"*Oui, mon chou.*"

He was evidently as intent on pleasing her as he was

myself. Perhaps his conscience took at the thought of how he had enjoyed me in her absence some months before. In a moment he returned bearing as beautiful a pair of boots as I had ever seen. The black kid leather was of the finest. The steel eyelets for the laces gleamed. The boots were of the full length I had been promised.

"Shall I try them on here?"

"No, there is not sufficient *confort*. My bedroom would be better. There is a larger mirror there."

The drapes on the bed as also the curtains and the lamps were mauve. Silver trinkets on the dressing table were numerous. I began to raise my skirt. M. Dalmaine hovered at the door.

"Close the door, Pierre, and draw the curtains. Mademoiselle does not wish to be seen. Light the lamps. Ah, but the dress is too heavy. Let me remove it for you."

I had attired myself of a purpose for the occasion. Beneath my dress I wore but a light chemise of pink batiste. The shade of my stockings and my garters matched it exactly. The hem of the chemise fell barely below my stocking tops. Madame Dalmaine's eyes gleamed. Her husband's were no less fervent.

"Be seated, Mademoiselle. The bed is *confortable, n'est-ce pas*? Extend your legs. Permit me to fit you."

I leaned back on my arms and extended first my right leg. My boots were delicately removed.

"*Alors*, the right one first, yes?"

My leg was raised higher. I affected to blush and turn my face away from Monsieur Dalmaine who was watching closely. As I drew up my knee, the hem of my chemise folded back. A glimpse of curls showed between my thighs. I covered myself coyly with the palm of my hand. The boot slid easily onto my foot and was smoothed upwards. It's passage seemed never-ending. Its fit over my knee was perfect. The softness and pliability of the leather was exquisite. In a moment Madame Dalmaine's hands had reached my thighs. The top of the boot came exactly within an inch of my stocking top.

"A little must always show above, Mademoiselle. It is more saucy, no?"

I lay back since there was nothing else to do.

"Such perfect skin! What whiteness of thighs, *mon dieu*!"

The left boot was fitted as sleekly. With a certain gallantry, Monsieur Dalmaine extended his hand and drew me up. I regarded myself in a full-length mirror. The effect was indeed delightful. The leather encased my legs tightly even to my thighs. Madame Dalmaine stood behind me.

"Raise your chemise, Mademoiselle, and you will get the full effect."

"Oh! but your husband!"

Too late. I was exposed both back and front. The chemise was held tightly to my waist. I sagged back against her to hide my bottom which was as naked as all beneath. A soft laugh greeted my coyness.

"They are boudoir boots, Mademoiselle—*pour le plaisir*! How sleek they feel! Pierre, feel her legs within them!"

I attempted a small struggle. Their hands upon me everywhere. For a bootmaker, M. Dalmaine seemed unaccountably excited by leather.

"No! Oh! What are you doing?"

My face was turned, my arms pinioned. Her lips smothered my cries. I absorbed her tongue as if I could not help but do so. Monsieur Dalmaine's hand dared to cup my slit. Raising my chemise to beneath my armpits his lips descended upon my nipples. I squirmed sufficiently to excite them both further. In a trice I was laid upon the bed. My thighs held open, my shoulders pinned, Madame began to tongue me. The ecstasy was exquisite. I bucked and moaned. Monsier Dalmaine presented the sturdiest of cocks to my hand. His kisses lavished themselves upon my mouth. I rubbed him gently.

Madame went about her business as slowly and deliciously as she had done before. Her tongue flickered and flicked. It entered and withdrew, sweeping upwards in long strokes around my clitoris. An insensate pleasure entered into me. In a moment the swollen crest of her husband's prick urged itself rudely between my lips. I sucked upon it as a child sucks upon a teat, caressing the shaft delicately. My hips bucked to the ministrations I was receiving from Madame's mouth and tongue. Twice I loosed a fine, salty rain which mingled with her saliva.

"*Fais-le-lui, Pierre! Plonges ton pine dedans!*"

The *pine* of Monsieur Dalmaine was now gross in size. It had swollen even more in my mouth. I moaned and tossed. They exchanged places. Straddling her knees about my shoulders, his wife raised her skirt.

"*Lêches-moi, mon ange*! Lick!"

I could scarce do other since her pale bottom had descended upon my face. A thick fringe of curles brushed my mouth. I tasted saltiness and musk. My tongue shot upwards between the oily lips even as the knob of his tool pressed its attention within my slit.

Madame bounced and squirmed until at moments I was all but smothered. The lips of her sex ground over my mouth in the most lascivious way. I gurgled and moaned as if taken by surprise still. The wicked penis of Monsieur Dalmaine had embedded itself full within me and was a perfect pleasure. It began to move, pistoning back and forth. I urged his efforts with subtle movements of my bottom. I squeezed upon his rod, sucking it deep within. The bed rocked.

The tip of my nose moved in the groove of Madame's

bottom. Every quiver of her delight transmitted itself to me. Twice her muffled cries of pleasure came as she loosed her spray upon my darting tongue. A second later and I was inundated with her husband's sperm.

"You enjoy, *hein*? The boots, they are exciting, *non*?"

I was kissed suavely by Madame while her husband with limply protruding penis rose to button the flap of his breeches. I made no reply. My eyes were as one astonished. I did not intend to let them enter into all my secrets.

"You enjoy again, perhaps? Pierre, *vas-t-en!*"

Obediently he departed. We were left alone.

"Do you treat all young women so?"

"Such pleasures are unfortunately rare, Mademoiselle. I judged you not loose, but perhaps tempted. The boots had the final effect, *n'est-ce pas*?"

Whether she was cunning or merely naive I knew not.

"Perhaps. I prefer to guide my own pleasures. You shall not take me by surprise again. What if I report you both?"

She sat up, truly alarmed. I enjoyed the expression in her face.

"Oh! Mademoiselle would surely not?"

"Not so long as you do as I say. My companion, Emma, will come later. Perhaps today or tomorrow. I find her irksome in her ways. She is not sophisticated, you understand? You will not persuade her as easily as you have done myself."

Her face had softened with relief. She bent over me. I permitted her to kiss me, though my response was faint. Her lips were as skilful as any woman's I have known. They moved softly back and forth in a butterfly touch across my own. I was stirred but showed it not. Another penis would have sufficed me better in that moment.

"She is *jolie*, that one, though not as you, Mademoiselle."

"Whether or not, you will treat her firmly. Are we understood?"

"I believe so. Ah! what I would not give for your tongue again. *Tu me léchais à merveille!*"

Her hand passed between my thighs. I was exceedingly sticky there with her husband's effusion. Her fingers soothed the oozing sperm over my thighs. It was warm still. The sensation was not unpleasant under her touch. Her tongue insinuated itself at last within my mouth. Her finger circled my button.

"What shall we do with her, Mademoiselle—this Emma?"

"A sound spanking if she will not stay still for the fittings. You will hold her over your lap and keep her so while your husband attends to her immediately you have finished smacking her."

"OH! I like!"

Her laugh was silvery. Our mouths joined anew. I parted my thighs wider.

"Come—you may pleasure me again now. Use your tongue. Do not stop until I tell you!"

Her compliance was immediate. I enjoyed myself to perfection. All that I lacked was the penis of the young rogue in the studio in my bottom.

"Emma, your boots are ready. They would like you to attend this afternoon. I called in there by chance. See—I have my own. Are they not splendid? Would you like to try them on?"

"Can you not come with me, Eveline?"

"Oh, what a baby you are! I have things to do. You must be very still during the fittings for they like to get this exact.

If you wriggle they will spank you, I am sure. Indeed, I was threatened with it for I am very ticklish, you know."

"Indeed? How ridiculous! Of course I would not let them do any such thing! I shall ask Papa to accompany me."

"That would do little good, my dear, for you must remove your outer attire first. No, I am but half joking. What a silly you are, but such a dear one! Did you enjoy your night? You have not said a word about it and dear Papa has not been in sight since last night. Did you exhaust him?"

Her colour rose high. I had hit upon one aspect of the truth at least. I doubted not that she had been mounted more than once.

"Eveline, do not speak of it! How ashamed I feel!"

I passed my arm about her. I drew her down on to a couch.

"What nonsense is this now? Ashamed? Did you not give and receive the most heavenly pleasure? Was it not you who lured me into these paths? No—do not speak, Emma, for I can see it in your eyes. Your modesty is as delightful as ever. Would that I could be as you. Oh, that we might one day share such transports together!"

"Oh, Eveline, how truly shameful!"

I had drawn her back and pressed my lips upon hers even as she spoke. Her mouth was small and succulent.

"Because your secret pleasures excite me and open up for me a world I had never dreamed of? Oh, but, Emma, sweet, let us talk of other things. Perhaps it will come to pass, perhaps not. Fate takes a hand in all these things, does it not? How you palpitate in my arms! What pleasures you must have known!"

"Do not speak of it! You said you would not!"

"Such pretty lips—such adorable eyes—such a perfect bust and exquisite legs. Oh, forgive me again, you do carry me away. OH!"

My exclamation was caused by the sudden entry of my uncle who gazed down upon us in our embrace and smiled. Emma immediately tried to free herself from my arms but I held her as if defensively.

"We were but talking, Uncle!"

"I deny it not. And kissing, too. A pretty sight as I ever saw. It becomes young ladies to show affection, does it not?"

I nodded, I laughed. I showed a merriment of spirit. With my arm still about Emma's shoulders I looked at her for reply.

"I don't know."

Her reply was muted, sullen, her expression foolish. I understood her better in that moment. Once firmly plugged she would surrender. Until then she would exhibit all her silly mannerisms.

"She does not mean it, Uncle. She is but shy. If we do not all show affection to one another the world is lost indeed. I swear she will be of merrier spirits at the ball tonight. Will you not, Emma?"

I laughed and drew her up. His arms enfolded both our slender waists.

"What will you do with us, Uncle?"

His response was as I had intended. Still holding us both tightly he pressed his mouth upon my own. While affecting to giggle I inserted my tongue against his own. My thigh pressed against a certain protuberance in his breeches. I felt it stiffen. Emma jerked and would have freed herself if I had not in turn pressed her to him. His arm loosed me. His hands pressed around her bottom. For a moment she could not escape the seeking of his fingers. Her cheeks flamed. Their mouths met briefly and she broke away.

"Oh! How silly!"

His condition was such by now as was evident even to her

eyes which had cast a sly look down and then averted themselves. Possessed as he was of a considerable weapon, its length and girth were outlined clearly through his breeches. The front of them strained considerably. Grinning at us both, he could not disguise the lewdness in his features as he turned and went out awkwardly.

I anticipated her objections.

"What harm, Emma? There was no one here to see. I must see to what I am going to wear tonight for the ball."

My tone was calm as if nothing had happened. Before she could reply I was gone.

"Have Alice sent up to me."

"Yes, m'am."

"Alice, will you like it here?"

"Oh yes, Miss, it's real heaven, that's what it is."

"Good. You have met the footman, John? He is a lusty fellow, but I want you to have none of him. I will have him married to Mary, though they do not know it yet."

I knew I could confide in her. Her reliance upon me was obvious.

She gazed at me with adoration.

"Yes, Miss. I won't let him do nuffink."

"Lord L. will see you on his return about your wages, Alice. He knows nothing of the photographic affair and is to be kept in ignorance of that or I fear it would disturb him. He believes me the most virtuous of maidens—you understand?"

"Nary a word, Miss, not to anyone. I won't tell a soul. All I wants to do is to please you and stay here, if you lets me."

"I will, Alice. Just keep your eyes and ears open. I may have things for you to do. There will be a ball tonight. Lord L. will speak to you on our return. If he wishes to engage you in a long conversation that will be to the good. I wish him to stay in his room and rest well. I shall expect you to see to that."

My tone was innocent, but I believe she understood.

"I'll do what I can, Miss."

"Go to the stables, Alice, and tell Jim there to have the carriage at the front again at two-thirty to take Miss Emma out."

A knock sounded. It was John.

"A Captain Richmond, Miss—a friend of your father's, but Lord L. is out."

"Very well, John, I will see him in the drawing room."

11

"*F*ORGIVE my disturbing you, Miss Eveline."

Captain Richmond was a spare, tallish man of some forty-five years. He wore a trim moustache but no beard. His scarlet and blue uniform of the First Yorkshire Cavalry suited him well. In speaking he had glanced quickly at my left hand. My wedding ring had been removed.

"Not at all. Papa may be some time, I fear. You must allow me to entertain you."

I rang for John. Whisky and soda was served to the Captain, wine for myself. He had only latterly returned from India, I understood. His sunbronzed complexion gave witness to that. I indulged him with girlish wonder, for he too had taken part in the battle of Muddipoor with my father. His adventures must have been legion, I said. Modesty preventing him on expanding upon them, I turned to other subjects. Indian ladies intrigued me. I had frequently wondered what they wore beneath their saris. I dared to venture the question.

"Little enough, if the truth be known."

His eyes had brightened at my mentioning the subject. Evidently he was more used to timid and entirely proper English girls. When naked and in privacy, he said, some Indian girls used scented oils upon their bodies. It made them more sinuous to the touch. Ayahs—nurses or companions—sometimes taught young English girls the art.

"To what purpose? That it provides easier lubrication, perhaps?"

My eyes were bold. He could not but perceive that. Seated as we were together on a sofa, his hand laid itself with avuncular jollity on my thigh. His fingers moved slightly but sufficiently to feel whether or not I was tightly gartered.

"Indeed, that would be the purpose of it. Young ladies frequently become very bored in the hills. They are soon guided by their ayahs to the amorous arts. Even at fifteen or sixteen they—like many Indian girl camp-followers—are prepared for the surreptitious caresses of the males."

"They remain not virgins at such ages?"

His eyes regarded me narrowly. His hand moved an inch higher and felt no doubt through my dress the transition from stocking to warm flesh. The crinkling of flesh around his eyes was devilishly attractive.

"Of a kind."

I wrinkled my nose as if endeavouring to ascertain his

meaning, though I had sensed already what he meant and felt an inner excitement rising in me. My facial expression, however, he took for disdain and quickly seized my hand.

"I meant not to shock you, Miss Eveline."

"The thought of such oils intrigues me, Captain. Can they not be obtained here in England?"

Our eyes met with a certain understanding.

"If you will permit, I have several phials in my case which lies in the hall."

"Very well—but it may not prove suitable to show them to me here. I shall be in my room. The door faces the stairs on the second floor."

Whether my invitation was totally indiscreet or not in relation to a companion-in-arms of Papa, I cared not. He had a sufficient look about him to ensure the tightest discretion. In a few moments he had joined me. I had poured liqueurs to ensure his comfort. The two phials of oil he handed me were no more than six inches long. I raised my eyebrows. He laughed.

"A little goes a long way. A smearing on the palm will cover most parts with ease."

"Or those which matter?"

"Indeed yes! Would you like to try?"

"Supposing I were a virgin and wished to remain so?"

"Then I will show you. The pleasure can be extreme."

"Really?"

My eyes laughed as did my mouth. In another second it accepted the salute of his.

"You must show me, Captain. I am a novice in this."

He led me to the bed, turned me about to face it and —without further ado—raised my skirt completely to my hips. I heard the intake of his breath at what he exposed.

"My God! What a beauty you are! Remain well bent, legs apart."

"Oh! what are you going to do to me? Is it my bottom, you mean?"

"Of course—and what a perfect apple you have, and so deeply split! It will take but a second or two to effect the lubrication. Only remain still for a while."

"Oh, your finger! How naughty you are! Ah! it is going right in, but it does not hurt. What a delicious perfume! OOOH! no more! I cannot stand it! AAAAH!"

I wriggled insensately. Well-oiled as it was, his forefinger had invaded me completely. As with the young man in the studio, I felt as if all the breath were being expelled from my body. I would have risen and thrust his hand away had his own left hand not clamped itself strongly on the back of my neck and held me over.

"Be still, little one! Many younger than you have struggled as much. When they become used to it they cannot get enough. It is impossible for them to become enceinte in this way and yet the pleasures they derive are undeniable!"

"You are hurting me! Take it out!"

In truth he was not. A fervid excitement had me as much in its grip as I was in his. My passage thoroughly eased, his finger moved teasingly back and forth. Finally he removed it and oiled with equal niceties of touch the lips of my slit beneath.

"What is that for? Oh please let me up!"

"When a girl is older she learns to have two up her at once. Lubricated as she is, the exercise literally sends her to heaven."

That was exactly what I now most desired, but I did not tell him so. His hand removed itself cautiously from the back of my neck. I did not move. I heard sounds behind me that were all too well known. He was divesting himself of jacket and trousers.

"Is this what you do to fifteen-year-old girls?"

My voice was broken off by the sudden conjunction of his loins to my upraised bottom. A considerable plum of swollen manhood urged against my well-oiled rose. A sound that was literally a snorting of pleasure escaped him as he urged it in. I yielded. My head swum. It was twice the size of the young man's, yet its entry, though pressing tightly against the interior, seemed no more difficult.

"My Adj . . . Adj . . . Adjutant has two fine girls—one fifteen, the other seventeen. By heavens how their bottoms have wriggled many a time to our pricks!"

"WHA-AAAAT? Oh! NO! That is too much! Take it out!"

My hips were gripped, my pleas ignored. Half inch by half inch he eased the big shaft in. I clawed at the bedcover. I moaned, I beseeched him. Little did he know the ecstasy he was affording me. I was stretched as never before. Every little throb and jerk of his weapon added to my sensations.

"Is it true? Did they really?"

I did not care about the answer—or the question. Nor could either of us have spoken in the next moment or two that it took him to slowly cork me to the full. For that, I learned, was the correct term among the officers in India.

I rested my cheek on my palms. Again all breath seemed to have deserted me, but now that feeling began to recede and I was overtaken by pleasure of a degree seldom known. My bottom encased his thick tool tightly. So closely in fact did I grip it that for long seconds he was unable to move. Then I relaxed. I had made my strength and eagerness known.

"Ah, you beauty, you little devil, have you not had this before?"

"Never! Ah! what a feeling it is! Draw it out and push it right up again. Not too fast!"

"You like it?"

Like all males he was glorying in the thought as much as in the act. For myself I needed only to savour the thrilling sensations that coursed through me.

"It hurts a little but it is nice."

"The hurting will soon pass, Eveline. Move your bottom only back and forth, but not sideways. Ah! you're as tight as any girl I ever had!"

"Go on! don't stop! You were right—it doesn't hurt now. Oh, but what a big one you have. Push it right in—let me feel it—AAAAAH! Do you like my bottom? Is it warm and tight?"

"Exquisite! Work your hips more! Ah! you are learning! How supple you are, what lovely bottom cheeks! I shall come in a minute!"

"Yes! do it in me! I want to feel it!"

His hand was around the front of my body. Probing fingers found my clitoris with all the skill of an old bedroom campaigner. Thrills coursed through me. I bounced my bottom repeatedly against his belly, forcing him in and out. I was dissolving in the spell of it. My climax spurted and spattered, flooding his fingers with my own liqueur while the powerful jets of his come throbbed and leapt up in me. Yes! Ah! I could feel every one. I could feel the throbbing of his knob, the splashing, the leaping. The sensation was delirious. When I last I subsided and he fell upon me, his root remained buried between my tight cheeks. We lay in panting quiet. I squeezed and felt the answering pulsing of his cock.

Reluctantly at last he withdrew it. A faint plop sounded. I rose immediately and inspected my prize. Though of half length now it was still of virile aspect. We kissed. I fondled it. It oozed its pearls upon my palm.

"I have initiated you!"

I hid my face in pretended coyness.

"You overwhelmed me, sir. I had not dreamed ever to do such a thing. How practised you are! Was it true about the Adjutant's daughters?"

"That we corked them both? By jove, yes. The younger squealed a good deal at the beginning, though she had been well coached by her ayah. Once fully plugged, then pleasure overtook her. Neither will go two or three days without their injections now. Such secrets are well-kept, Eveline."

I concealed my eyes.

"I am sure they must be. How perfectly wicked. I would love to have seen it. What mornings or afternoons you must have had!"

"Only in the night, Eveline, for the heat is too stifling by day. Dawn is as good a time as any. The girls were always bottom-warm between the sheets by then. Drowsy as they sometimes were, they took the double salute like angels, and like angels went back to sleep again. By breakfast time you would have taken them for innocents still."

"I do not doubt—and no signs to show for it, as you say. But now we must take haste to return down or our absence will be noted. Go first and quickly and I will follow."

Emma, I learned, had departed for the bootmakers. The thought of what she was by then experiencing added a trifle to my pleasures.

"You must come to the ball tonight, Captain."

"I fear I cannot, dear Eveline, for my wife, who advanced to England before me, is expecting my return. She is not much given to dancing. Tell your Papa only that I called. We shall meet again?"

"In circumstances no less agreeable to both parties, I am sure."

I fondled his tool which had grown again somewhat

during our conversation. Our embrace became passionate and would have resulted in a "double salute" had I not feared the servants' approach.

"I am sure you will preserve it for me, Captain."

"Of that you may have no doubt, Eveline. England is already beginning to look as fair as India was."

I escorted him into the hall. Descending the stairs, Alice glanced at us and then hurried on. I would have to teach her that she must never look directly in passing unless spoken to. Her passage attracted the Captain's eye. He turned to gaze after her. The little minx waggled her bottom, I sensed, on purpose.

"My goodness, Eveline! What a delightful little creature!"

"MY goodness she would no longer be if I allowed you to entertain her bottom, Captain."

He gazed at me with quizzical eyes. I could not help but smile at his expression. Not many men amuse me by meaning to.

"There is no hope?"

"Perhaps a little. We shall see."

His mixture of gallantry and humour, tinged with the commanding manner in which he had bent me over, afforded me amusement. The sensation of our mutual enjoyment lingered in my bottom still. Discarding the conventions, I waved to him in his departing carriage from the front door. I returned then to my liqueurs. I had much to think about. It was a full hour and a half before Emma returned.

"You look *distrait*, Emma. Did the boots fit? Oh, my goodness, how your hair is mussed! There is a high wind outside, I imagine."

"Oh, Eveline! I cannot bear to tell you! Those horrid people! I shall report them—I shall tell Papa!"

"Tell? What have you to tell? What is the matter?"

"I was assaulted, and so rudely! I cannot bear to relate what happened."

"Then you will not be able to report it, silly. Tell me and I will tell your papa. That will save you embarrassment."

"No! I dare not!"

"Then what is to do if no one knows what you are talking about? Come upstairs. We shall have privacy. Tell your Eveline all."

The story was soon dragged from her. It was as I hoped. The Dalmaines had acted to perfection. Monsieur Dalmaine had given her a full injection while she squirmed and tossed across his wife's lap.

"Oh, Emma! Did you not encourage them but a little? First John and then Papa! Am I to tell Uncle all this and betray your trust in me? Do you not realise that he would drag it all from me?"

"Please do not! Oh please do not! It is all true, I swear, but Papa must never know."

In her excitement and with much wringing of her hands she had cast herself at my feet. I lay back upon my bed. Her arms enfolded my legs. Her sobs were somewhat theatrical. I would soon extract from Madame Dalmaine what pleasure Emma had evinced during the little orgy. Perhaps she knew that.

"Then you must do as I say, Emma—implicitly and without question."

"I will, I will! Oh, Eveline, I promise."

I drew my legs from her grasp and, before she realised what I was about to do, placed them over her shoulders, hooking my knees over them.

"You have all the pleasures, Emma. It is I who languish here. No—do not speak. I have done all I can for you. I have intrigued and lied for you. It is my turn now. Eveline is frustrated, Emma. Raise my skirt and kiss me there."

Somewhat miraculously she obeyed. Baring me to my waist while I kept my legs about her, she nuzzled with lips and tongue the very spot I most desired to have titillated after the Captain's other attentions.

"Lick faster, Emma, around the spot! Oh, divine girl, how nicely you do it! Ah, I am in heaven!"

Even then I did not forget the flattery which was as water to the sponge of her spirit. A few further flickers of her tongue and such was my pent-up excitement that I came in a rare flood over her lips. A languor seized me. My legs slipped down. Emma rose and lay timidly beside me. I stirred, I lay upon my hip and faced her.

"You have pleased me, Emma, my sweet cousin. Have I not constantly told you how skilled in the amorous arts you have become?"

I stroked her cheeks, I kissed her. She softened more and more in my arms and finally lay relaxed. Why I wished to treat her in this way I no longer knew. Perhaps it was the excitement of witnessing her constant surrenders. Had she been of livelier spirits generally I would have let her go her own way. As it was she presented a challenge. The need to break her into total submission was paramount.

I licked the salt of my effusions from her tongue.

"Was the bootmaker's cock a good one, Emma?"

"Oh yes—no!—oh, you shouldn't ask!"

"*YES* is sufficient, my pet, for I know by now your thoughts. Before you leave you shall have the same that you so deliriously received in Papa's bed."

She started visibly. Her blush was deep. It spread down to her neck.

"But your papa . . ."

"Was absent, Emma. Did you not think I would discover

that? I was deceived even as you. But half an hour after you entered the bedchamber I learned of Papa's absence. Quivering with disbelief I awaited your flight into my own room. You did not reappear, Emma!"

"OH!"

Her voice was a single wail. I silenced it with my lips.

"How naughty you truly are, Emma."

"B . . . b . . . but, Eveline!"

"You will do as I say, Emma."

I rose. I adjusted my gown. Seating myself at my dressing table I fussed with my locks. The silence was as complete as I desired. In a moment she rose and hesitantly began to make her exit.

"I mean what I say, Emma!"

"Oh!"

She squealed and was gone. The door slammed.

I was not deceived.

12

"PERCY, dear boy, I had least expected you now!"

The appearance of my brother surprised and pleased me even though I was half an hour away from departing to the ball. We had met but once since my marriage and now, elevated to the rank of Captain in his regiment, he looked exceedingly fine and handsome in his uniform of scarlet and gold braid.

"You must come to the ball, Percy. It would be great fun."

We had exchanged our compliments and news. I said nothing of my plans. Only Papa knew of them.

"How adorable you look, Evie, in your white dress. How soft the satin feels!"

We stood in the music room, locked in an embrace from which I did not attempt to stir. My episode with my cousin had excited me to a considerable extent. Percy's hot lips covered mine.

"Do you go without drawers still, Evie?"

"Oh, for shame, Percy! No, do not raise my skirts —someone may come in!"

"How I have dreamed to fondle your warm furry little mound once more, my sweet. Come, show me your beautiful legs again at least. What curves, what slenderness, what a beautiful view!"

"Ah! do not! You are crushing me. Be careful or you will ruin my stockings!"

Not since my wedding day had Percy "presented his compliments" to me, having sworn to have me again first after that event, as he had said. I had succumbed then, arrayed as I still was in my wedding gown. The fact that my ball dress was also white excited his memories the more.

The pale of my thighs gleamed above the shimmering silk of my stockings. He made bold to lay me back upon a convenient sofa. His kisses covered my face. I murmured my protestations all too softly. In but a moment I held his cock in my hand. Our tongues dallied.

"It grows ever bigger, Percy, I swear!"

"The very thought of you distends it mightily, my love. Part your darling legs wider now!"

"Oh, Percy!"

He was upon me and in. His "compliments" were as exciting as they had been long months before. My bared bottom moved luxuriously on the brocaded surface of the sofa which tickled me nicely. Another second and his balls hung beneath my hemispheres.

"Percy, oh! You excite me madly! Do not come too soon —your Evie wants to enjoy it."

"My darling! Ah, my sweet sister! How tight and soft you are! Give me your tongue—uncover your breasts! How delicious your nipples look! How long it must have been since you enjoyed a bout!"

"Yes, Percy—so long!"

His shaft moved in my velvet grip. I worked my bottom gently. His belief in my innocence was ever pleasing. Percy had never asked me about my wickednesses. He believed himself, I think, to be one of my very few conquerors.

We sucked upon each other's tongues. Our loins threshed faster. The exquisite moment would be upon us soon. Raising one leg I coiled it about his buttocks and pressed the heel of my shoe into him imploringly.

"Oh! what am I letting you do, Percy—how naughty we are!"

" 'Tis the perfect sin, Evie. Your supple body excites me madly. How your slit sucks upon my cock! Oh, you delicious girl!"

He groaned, he panted. His manly form covered me. I clutched his shoulders and drummed with my heel upon his buttocks. I sobbed my pleasure.

"Come in me, Percy—I want it all!"

Divine shudders seized us. Our mouths locked. All that I had spoken of with Papa was present in this delirious moment in the exquisite conjunction of our parts. Percy's cock throbbed the more in me. It slewed back and forth. I gripped him tightly. The sofa creaked beneath us. A hollow croak from my brother announced his end. The long jets of his sperm entered and swam in me. I returned the compliment by wetting his cock and balls the more. Our tongues moved faster in the final delirium. Then we sank down.

"Naughty boy, it has dripped all over my stockings, I will have to change. Emma is descending now, I think. Make haste—cover yourself—entertain her while I am gone."

My disorder was all too evident. By chance I avoided my cousin who went first in search of me into the drawing room. Ascending the stairs I encountered my uncle. I had tripped in going down, I told him. I doubted that he believed me. Entering my room immediately behind me he seized and kissed me. Had he attempted then to raise my skirt he would have found me literally foaming with Percy's sperm.

"Wait! We shall have a chance perhaps at the ball, Uncle."

"You mean it?"

"There may be more privacy. I know of an alcove which is often discreetly screened. We may enjoy ourselves there, if you wish. You will bring your big key? Oh dear, it seems larger now—have you been oiling it?"

He had the grace to flush. His hands explored my breasts, which were half exposed. My nipples tingled to his thumbs. He dared not venture to ask what I knew.

"You will not wear drawers tonight, Eveline?"

"No more than Emma. Go now or we may be discovered. The alcove, remember. You will see a Chinese screen in front of it. At ten I shall go within."

His eyes were as hot with expectancy as his penis was prominent in his breeches. Closing the door I changed both my stockings and garters. I had used my words with him carefully. A devil of mischief was within me. Drawing Percy to one side when I returned downstairs I apprised him of my plan—or at least that part of it which it would be convenient for him to know about.

"Evie! I never thought it of you!"

"Nor I, Percy, but it is her secret wish. She has confessed it to me. The dear girl is in a perfect lather for it."

"Have no doubt, Evie, that I shall see she gets it. Leave all to me."

On the steps of the Claremont I encountered Captain Richmond who was accompanied by a rather timid-looking woman of his own age. I guessed her immediately to be his wife. The Captain and I nodded as formal acquaintances. Introductions were effected. By good fortune then Percy engaged himself in conversation with Mrs. Richmond. I was able to draw her husband briefly aside. It needed but a moment or two to effect my news.

"In the alcove, you say? By jove!"

"At nine forty-five, Captain—a rare little treasure. Have no nonsense with her for she secretly adores the thought."

I turned back immediately to his wife. In moments, upon our entering, Percy had entered his name upon her dance card exactly at the time I wished. Emma, flanked by Papa and her father, looked all a-flutter at the dazzling scene within. The chandeliers glittered, the band played a waltz. We were all soon on the floor. I kept close account of the time. Plied with pink champagne laced with an occasional glass of wine, Emma entered one of her merriest moods.

Some indiscretions among the assembly were already evident. Palm trees surrounding the ballroom provided cover for those who sought it. Many a pair of lips were kissed and bottoms fondled as partners broke off momentarily to take shelter. Emma could not help but have her attention drawn to it.

"Shall we watch, Emma? Look, there is a corner where we can hide."

Protesting as was always her wont, she was drawn there. The quicker beating of her heart was evident to me as we watched a couple in passionate embrace. The man's hand groped up beneath the lady's skirt, revealing as fine a plump pair of thighs as one might wish to see. Her fingers engaged themselves with the front of his breeches. Conveying my excitement to Emma, I kissed her.

"There is one here who would embrace you also, Emma—a handsome devil of a man."

"Oh? Who? Tell me, Cousin!"

"I dare not mention his name, my sweet. He languishes for you. D'you see that alcove over there, fronted by a lacquered screen? Be there in five minutes. Slip behind the screen. No one will see you. I will keep guard. Hasten now and be ready to take your place. I will divert your Papa."

I hustled her forth. A secret engagement of such nature was one that no woman could resist. Percy accepted the signal of my handkerchief. Gazing about herself in a flurried manner, Emma finally disappeared behind the screen. Any shriek that she might have uttered was concealed beneath the noise of the orchestra and the general humming of voices. Shrieks were not infrequent on such occasions, in any event.

I skirted the dancers and accosted my uncle. It was nigh on the hour of our appointment. I stepped before him.

"Have you seen Emma?"

"No."

He frowned and looked about. My question must have appeared frivolous in the tension of his waiting.

"No matter. I shall just tell Papa that I shall be absent for a short while. Give me a few seconds and follow."

I made the interval longer while he fretted and fumed. A full two minutes passed before I ventured the screen. Someone passed me as I did so, his face all aglow. It was Captain Richmond. Idling close by in discreet concealment, Percy gave me a nod. I would gain from him later the full details of how, entering the dark alcove, Emma had been seized between the two of them. Her mouth and bottom had suffered their dual assault, though she had not known who either were.

My eyes accustomed themselves to the dim light. Emma lay awry upon a small red velvet couch, her skirts well up. The stickiness about her mouth was as nothing to that which trickled slowly down the backs of her thighs. Somewhat glazed in her expression she encountered my eyes precisely at the moment that her father entered behind me, his cock rampant at the thought of the pleasures that awaited him.

Emma would have shrieked sufficiently then to drown the band had I not with caution muffled her cry.

"Oh, Emma!"

"Papa! Eveline!"

The evidence was not to be hid, quickly as she made to cover her legs and bottom. I doubted even so whether my uncle would guess the nature of the rude Captain's entry. I pretended considerable shock. I raised her from the couch and clasped her to me.

"Uncle! there is but one thing to do! Summon a carriage!"

So dazed was he that he obeyed on the instant. Emma was quickly bundled out. No one of consequence noted our passing. Quite speechless, Emma could say nothing lest in my own indiscretion I also said too much. Nor had the hump in my uncle's breeches subsided. Its evidence was plain. The jolting of the carriage exacerbated his condition. Affecting confusion as we jolted over the cobbles in descending the Haymarket, I clutched it as if to steady myself.

"What is to do now, Uncle? There is but one thing."

I whispered in his ear. His face grew the more flushed. He nodded gravely. My fingers lingered a moment about his tool. Emma could not but help see the gesture as our carriage was illumined by the lights of the drinking dens we passed.

"Oh! what is to happen!"

"All shall be well, dear Emma. The possible effects of your wickedness must be neutralised, and within the hour, or you may become enceinte. A second dosage will suffice. The spermatic effusion will so mingle with the first that you will be safe."

"OH! I shall die first! How dare you say such things before Papa!"

"It is you, dear Emma, who have wantonly indulged yourself. Has she not, Uncle?"

Our mutual hypocrisies were such that I doubted any of us believed the other. In her perfect ignorance, however, my cousin was quite prepared to believe in what I had said about the mingling of the male effusions. Perhaps she even thought that she might become enceinte by virtue of the unconventional salute which Captain Richmond had given her. Her confusions hid beneath the cupping of her gloved hands over her face, she was led upon our arrival up to my room.

"Miss Emma has been taken poorly, John. See that we are not disturbed."

"Certainly, Miss Eveline."

Adopting a grave mien, my uncle escorted us within. Emma could not scream. Indeed, I believe she was incapable of doing so. With pretended sobs she allowed herself to be stripped and laid upon my bed. I divested myself of my gown and lay with her in my stockings. Gloating upon the spectacle we thus presented together, my uncle was not slow to offer himself in an equal state of Nature. His standing penis looked immense, the purplish knob positively glowing.

Emma, with closed eyes, clutched at me. Her small cries would have sounded piteous had I not known her better.

"No, Eveline! Oh, Papa! No, I dare not!"

Rolled swiftly upon her back, she offered the altar of desire—a fine puff of curls about her mount, her nipples rigid from the swooping assault of my lips. Sobbing and clasping me wildly she felt her thighs parted as he knelt over her.

"It is for your best, Emma. It must be done."

Her bottom rose from the coverlet, hips bucking. She was held. A groan of pure joy escaped him as he descended upon her. The crest of his swollen staff brushed her silken belly. It nudged the curls of her slit.

"No! Oh, Papa!"

I seized one of her legs beneath her knee and raised it, the better for him to effect his entry. His large hands seized her hips, quelling her jerks. A long shrill cry bubbled from her mouth. The huge plum slipped inside. The moist lips of her lovemouth closed about it. His balls swung like a bullock's as he urged it slow within. A quivering seized her. Her eyes rolled, her head falling flat on the pillow. For a moment her face twisted wildly from side to side and then with a grunt he was lodged full within.

"AH! how tight, how soft! How she clenches!"

"Move it powerfully and deep, Uncle. You must flood her fully or all will be lost! Assist him, Emma—move your bottom! Did you not say what a fine one he had?"

Her mouth was open. His own seized upon it. Her eyes, which had been but a moment before wide open, were now half-closed. She seemed lost to all but the sensation, as well she might. The working of their tongues showed clearly in the movements of their cheeks. Cupping her bottom with both palms he began to ram his tool back and forth in earnest.

I sat up. I was spectator to their divine pleasure. Emma's legs faltered, moved and then wound themselves up about his hips. Their bellies smacked together. The faint sluicing back and forth of his cock sounded in her lovenest. Its lips ringed the pestle tightly.

I fell beside them again and seized her mouth.

"Oh, Emma!"

"Eveline! AH!"

"Emma, he is touching me! Oh, I cannot but do it, too! Oh yes, go faster, yes!"

To whom I spoke mattered not. My bare hip rubbed against Emma's. A madness of pleasure seized us. His fingers busied themselves about my slit. I jerked my bottom in response. Our three tongues licked together in the wantonness of our posture. His groans resounded. A fine spray upon his hand announced my own excitement.

"Ah, I am coming—coming, Emma!"

"P . . . P . . . Papa, yes! More, more—oh more!"

The bed, large as it was, trembled and shook. The very ecstasy of the angels was upon us. The bedcover was inundated in our violent tremors. Panting and working our tongues she received his all. Trembling from our exertions we collapsed and huddled together.

"Draw down the bedcovers, Uncle. Shall we not make ourselves more comfortable? The deed is done. Let us enjoy ourselves all the more."

Limp and quiescent, Emma was drawn between us beneath the sheet. While kissing her I passed my hand across and dandled his prick. Limp as it then was, it remained eager, I knew, to raise its head again. Turning Emma on her hip towards me, I brought her bottom to bulge against it.

Stirring it gently, she brought her tongue to enter my mouth.

Emma, it seemed, was converted at last.

13

*B*OOTED and in the tiny stays which I had at last acquired without further assault from their designer, I preened myself in my mirror.

The effect was indeed electric. Precisely as Madame Dalmaine had said, my gartered stocking tops rose but an inch above the rims. Between the garters and the lower edge of the waist corset, all was displayed. I fluffed the curls of my mount and smiled my pleasure. They appeared to have thickened, presenting a more luxuriant growth after the many waterings they had received of late.

Emma had departed two days before. I regretted nothing.

In converting her I had but ripped another banner of pretence from the false facade that Society had erected. The pleasures of lust had risen full to the surface in her at last. She was free to enjoy, even as I. Voltaire's little lesson upon the pleasures of Charlemagne with his daughters had never been lost on me.

"We may rely upon your discretion, Eveline?" my uncle had asked upon the morning of their departure. Emma stood silent in the background. Her expression held a composure it had never known before. A sense of assurance had entered her. The lustiness of his loins was hers to command. I had no doubts that he would fête her considerably during the three days of their journey back.

"Of what is there to speak, Uncle? I had thought never to throw myself into such pleasures. Truly you have changed all that I ever thought. Hypocrisies have been cast down, all webs of deceit banished. You have taught me between you to enjoy. My debt is great to you."

His eyes searched my face even as did hers. Truly he believed me. He laughed.

"It is well said, Eveline. Come, Emma, kiss your cousin."

She advanced towards me. Our eyes met in a complicity of understanding. A merriment of relief at what I had said danced in her eyes. Perhaps she had thought it possible that I would reveal her other secrets. The brief passage of time had already veiled the little plots whereby I had inveigled her into such deeds. Her lips brushed mine suavely, all the better tutored after the several nights of pleasuring she had received. Even so I knew her better than she knew herself. Once back within the fold her newfound resolutions of pleasure would falter. Her boots and corsets would lie unused. She would need the birch again.

I said nothing of all this. Treated as a queen, she

departed. The curtain upon that little private theatre descended. A year later she married and settled down into a life of dullness. The strange surroundings of London and my own guile had been her only spur. Entertaining the parental pestle less and less and becoming pettish and moody once more, she sought refuge in the very conventions I had endeavoured to remove her from.

I wanted no more of her. I cast her from my mind. The future was my only concern. My lord had written but one letter to me, vaguely seeking some date of my return. I had replied with care. His emotions had never been entirely revealed to me. Our physical passions had never been of the uttermost.

I removed my boots. Papa had yet to see them. I had no doubt that they would drive him wild with desire, languishing as he frequently had in the touch of my kid gloves. I needed excitement such as at that moment even he could not afford me.

"John, summon my carriage."

"Will you go out this late, Miss Eveline? Shall you not want an escort?"

"Jim will defend me if I need it. I shall remain with the carriage. The night air will do me good. Have Sippett tell Lord L. that I am abed and asleep if he asks."

The air was sultry and warm. I had no idea of where to go and finally settled on the Café de Paris. Unusual as it was for a young woman to enter there alone, I was known sufficiently well to be guided to a table.

"Your escort will follow, Mademoiselle?"

"Perhaps."

I gave the head waiter a cool look and deposited a five pound note by my plate. He picked it up with some alacrity. There would be no further questions. A trio at an adjoining table had attracted my attention already. The woman of the three was in her early twenties. Her male companions, neither of whom had a military look, appeared but a trifle older.

My casual look engaged her own. No sooner had I started on my entree than the taller of the two men came solicitously towards me.

"Forgive me if I intrude. You appear to be alone. May I make so bold to ask if you would care to join us at dinner?"

I gazed past him towards the girl. She winked. It was a common gesture, but it amused me. Dressed as finely as she was, she was evidently not a lady.

"My escort appears to be delayed. Yes, I will join you."

A fresh entree was served. We sat four at table. A marble column hid us somewhat from the throng. The man who had approached me had a brash sort of confidence. The other, slimmer of figure, was quieter. We exchanged pleasantries. I was eager to see their game. It was not long in being revealed.

"We intend to have fun tonight—a bit of a lark. If your escort ain't coming, you could join us if you wished."

Her eyes sought assent in mine. I answered her as she desired. She was a town girl, fairly new to the streets, but had done well in her first ventures as her clothes and jewels evinced. Her escorts were the sons of Lords, she said. I pretended interest, knowing very well they were not. Their accents spoke of city merchants, spoiled sons of the *nouveau riche* who were currently endeavouring to invade Society.

"I don't mind but I have to be home by midnight."

"Time and enough. We're going to rooms round near Leicester Square. A couple of minutes walk will do it. Long as you feel larky you'll be all right. Bit of a lady yourself, ain'tcher?"

"Of sorts perhaps."

Her name was Sarah. The quieter of the two men was Edward, the other presenting himself as Fred. Beneath the tablecloth his hand made first acquaintance with my thighs. I did not move. The meal became rather hurried. To the despair of the waiter we did not indulge in a sweet. A different kind of indulgence was uppermost in our minds.

The rooms of which Sarah had spoken, and which like so many others were hired by the hour or the night, consisted of a small parlour and a bedroom. Sarah commenced to strip without ado. In a trice all four of us were naked. Lying back upon the bed she presented me with the very opportunity I required. They would have made to mount us side by side if I had not seized their cocks.

"Wait! I want both at once."

"Oh, you dirty thing! Are you going to have one in your mouth, Evie?"

Sarah sat up, looking quite put out. Perhaps she thought I was going to rob her not only of her due but her earnings.

"Lie on your back, Frank. Let me mount you. Would you like to put it in that way?"

He needed no second request. His penis stuck up like a flagpole. I straddled him and clasped it by seizing it from below and behind me. The big nut pushed upwards between my lips. I sighed and rotated my bottom, sinking down as slowly as I could.

"Frank, it is lovely! Push right up! AH!"

"What a pet you are—how warm and tight! Ah, what heaven! Move your bottom up and down!"

"Wait, Frank!"

I leaned forward, exposing my bottom.

"Now, Edward! I want a double one—come on!"

I was in a perfect rapture as he positioned himself. The lips of my slit tightened in anticipation around the root of

Frank's pulsing tool. Edward's smaller knob presented itself to my rosehole.

"Oh my God, I have never done this before, Evie!"

"Edward, go slowly, for I do not know if I can bear it yet! A little at a time—yes! Ah, no, not so quick!"

Frank was jerking frenetically beneath me. The thought that I was to be sandwiched between them excited him almost as much as the sensations I was sustaining. My breasts wobbled against his bare chest.

"Be still for a moment, Frank, or we shall not succeed. Oh! Edward! I can feel you! More, yes—a little more. AAAAAH! you are splitting me! Go on, go on!"

My senses swirled. Sarah, a pale form beside us, was forgotten. The throbbing in my loins was almost too delicious to contain. Gripping the whole doughty length of Frank's cock within me so that our pubic hairs brushed and intermingled, I received in my bottom more than half of Edward's.

I snorted in my passion. I writhed and twisted. Berserk with lust, young Edward rammed me to the root. I had both! I contained them! Their two lances throbbed in unison. I could scarce speak. An incomprehensible bubbling issued from my lips. Sarah's excited breathing sounded with my own and that of my two stallions. I jolted, I cried, I sobbed with pure pleasure as each in turn commenced moving his weapon back and forth.

"Oh, Evie, what a bottom! What heat, what clenching! What a delicious girl you are!"

Frank's compliments were no less. Such obscenities flew forth from us as befitted the triple act. Turn by turn their cocks entered and withdrew. Plugged or corked as I had been by Captain Richmond I suffered no agonies but only a delicious itching sensation with each ramming of Edward's tool. Its entry made my slit so tight that Frank could only throb within until his partner's was eased back, permitting him movement in turn. Jolting I gasped. Gasping I jolted. My tongue entered Frank's mouth. We exchanged divine kisses.

"More! Oh more—both of you!"

My desires were such that I would have had them continue forever. Frank, who possessed the bigger weapon, was the first to spill. His groanings sounded under my mouth. I received the leapings of his sperm. I clenched, I gripped, I implored more.

"Edward! do not stop! Both of you!"

Alas, Frank's now limper cock slipped almost from my grip. Mounding my bottom into Edward, I rotated it wildly.

"Do it to me! Let it come! OH! I can feel it! Yes, YES! Oh, what a flood!"

A moment more and the divine crisis had passed. My pubic hairs had matted with Frank's in the energy of my spillings. I collapsed upon him, panting. Withdrawing his long cork, Edward flopped beside us. I was wet in all my parts. I squeezed my bottom cheeks together, savouring the trickle of come from my rosette.

"Evie, you devil! I never thought it could be done! I ain't never had it up my bottom, though, and never likely to."

Whatever Sarah did or didn't interested me least in that moment. I rolled from Frank and lay silent. I had reached the peak of pleasure, one so rare that few women ever attain such voluptuous heights. My entire body pulsed with pleasure.

Remembering at last the time, I rose by the greatest effort and passed a napkin between my thighs and around my bottom. Frank and Edward were not to be revived for a while, however skilful Sarah might prove. Despite the protestations of the young "gentlemen," I drew my robe on once more, Sarah regarding me curiously but anxiously.

Her relief when I went to the door, having asked nothing for my "services" was evident.

Edward scrambled off the bed.

"Wait, Evie! Don't go yet? Where do you live?"

I was gone. In the bustling crowds around Leicester Square with its stinking heaps of garbage thrown out from the eating houses, two men made to clutch at my sleeve. I cast them off, snapping at them fiercely. I wanted not my thoughts of the pleasure I had sustained to be disturbed. Jim waited for me with the carriage in a side street.

"Have you eaten, Jim? You have not stayed with the horses all this time?"

"No, Miss, I went to a coffee house like you told me. Here's the change out of the guinea you give me."

"You may keep it, Jim. You are a good fellow. Let me down before we reach the house. I want to go in quietly."

My wishes were not fulfilled. A part of my life was about to be shattered, though the greater proportion of it was to prove fulfilled.

"Lord L. wishes to see you, Miss Eveline. He is in his room."

"Very well, Sippett. I am thirsty. Have a bottle of champagne brought up."

It was an unusual hour for Papa to summon me to his room. I ascended quickly, some premonition floating within me. Attired in a silk dressing gown he was pacing back and forth. At my entrance he drew me immediately to the bed. We sat upon it, his arm enfolded my shoulders.

"Papa, what is the matter?"

"I have the gravest news, Eveline. My little girl must be brave."

"Papa? Oh, tell me! I cannot bear suspense!"

"It is of Lord Endover, my love. A grave tragedy. The

news has only just reached me. A shooting accident, I fear. The poor fellow. Nothing could be done."

"Oh, Papa!"

I was truly shocked. I cast myself closer in his arms, my heart palpitating. The letter of parting I had been slowly devising in my mind need now not be written. Our marriage had but lasted a few months and while I had not truly known such sweetness and passion as I had sought, there was a companionship of sorts that was broken now forever.

A knock sounded. Sippett entered with champagne and another bottle.

"I thought as at you receiving the news, Miss, you might want a touch of brandy."

"Thank you, Sippett. I shall go to my room in a moment. Poor Lord Endover!"

Tears trickled down my cheeks. Papa kissed them away. A dosage of brandy helped a little to revive my spirits. Thoughts of all my wanton adventures during my absence from my husband passed like clouds through my mind, yet I upbraided myself not. He had found me not a virgin and yet had never asked of such things. He was given little to lewdness. His companions were invariably male. Whether he thought me an angel or a devil, I had never known.

"You will stay now, Eveline? There will not be time for you to reach Lord Endover's estate in time for the—ah—internment, I fear."

"Yes, Papa, if you will have me. I thought to buy a small cottage, perhaps in Sussex. It would make a pleasant retreat. Somewhere close to Eastbourne, perhaps, so that one can reach the coast also."

I concealed my smile. I accepted the glass of champagne that was proffered. Papa would not have forgotten our first trip to Eastbourne, though it was scarce time to think about it, nor to drink champagne.

"You must not be alone tonight, Eveline, or you will fret too much."

"Sippett will think it strange if I do not go to my room, Papa."

"She will be abed herself soon. Lie quiet. You must not let your thoughts stir too much."

"No, Papa."

I lay back. My legs dangled over the edge of the bed. Our lips met in an infinity of understanding. A tenderness seized us. My petal lips rolled back beneath his own. A distinct tremor was felt between us.

"Not now, Papa, it would be too wicked."

I stirred from his arms. He made no attempt to detain me. My parting smile was of the sweetest and most forlorn. In my bed I cast myself down and buried my face in the pillow. The future was opening up again before me.

I wanted it.

14

I CURTAILED my wearing of mourning after a month. Mourning should exist within one. It does not truly manifest itself in the constant wearing of black —though it suited me. Much evidence of that came to me in the many admiring glances I received. Even my garters, which few enough had opportunity to see, were of broad black lace adorned with tiny red rosettes. A single strand of strong elastic through the middle caused the lace to fluff out prettily above and below.

My search for a country retreat had begun. I appointed agents. With the death of Lord Endover I had come into a considerable fortune. My independence was now my own. Details of properties for sale reached me daily. One in particular attracted my attention. It was a three bedroom cottage on the edge of Ashley Forest, but half an hour's brisk trot by carriage from Eastbourne. It commanded several acres of ground which would ensure my privacy.

"Will it not be rather small, Eveline. It seems but a hovel in terms of size."

"Indeed no, Papa, for I mean not to entertain there in the given sense of the term. There is a private road before one reaches the drive. All comings and goings would thus be hidden from the sight of the villagers. The aspect beyond the cottage—if I read the description perfectly—is of forest and the downs. Can you think of a more pleasant view at early morning? I intend to place a deposit on it and then we shall see it. I have many plans for such a place."

"May I, too, not place a deposit, Eveline?"

I laughed. We were alone in his study. His errant hand sought my skirt and raised it sufficiently to seek the warm surfaces of my thighs.

"Oh, naughty Papa, you shall not place your deposit there —I am on my last day of mourning. No, Papa, desist!"

"What a pretty little treasure it is! I swear the curls have thickened. Part your legs, my darling, for I am in a very agony to see it again."

"No, Papa, the poor thing has been quite unattended this past month or so and has closed its lips to receiving any presents. By tomorrow, I expect, it will be pouting for attention. You must have patience indeed."

I had desisted, it was true, from any little adventures. Never had I been so virginal since the age of seventeen when I had first received the hunchback's teaspout in Paris. The torment however had been quite delicious. I had lived in anticipation of all that would transpire. As for Papa, he literally snorted to engage me in transports of lust, but I was adamant. The fact that he had in wise and gentlemanly fashion not attempted to enter my boudoir would serve only to increase his virility.

"But one kiss there, my pet!"

"A little one, then."

I rose from his lap. Raising my skirt anew I stood with thighs apart—a very vision of lewdness in my gartered black stockings and black dress. With a groan he fell before me to his knees. His nostrils twitched at the delicious perfumes I exhaled. That from between my thighs attracted him most. I steadied my legs. I shifted my heels apart a little more. My belly gleamed its silky splendour. Beneath was arrayed a fine, trim triangle of bushy curls.

"Oh! your moustache tickles, Papa!"

Clasping the backs of my thighs he nuzzled me for what was doubtless for him a blissful moment. His tongue protruded, lapping about the very lips which had forsaken his command. I quivered in my being. My knees bent. The gentle working of his tongue was exquisite. The tip reached upwards and touched my button.

"Ah! Papa, desist! Oh, what sensations you give me!"

He would have risen and clasped me had I not retreated quickly. Before he could get to his feet the study door had closed behind me.

The offices of the house agents, Smethers and Withers, lay but a short drive from the house. The door was curtained. I entered quietly. The front office where visitors were received was empty. A door which led to the inner sanctum beyond was ajar. A sound drew me to it. It was not such as one was accustomed to hearing in a place of business. Convinced that my ears were deceiving me completely I drew closer. The gap between the edge of the door and its surround was some eight inches. I perceived all.

Lying with her back upon the desk, which had evidently been cleared for battle, was a woman of some thirty years whom I had seen before. She assisted the partners in their clerical work. At the moment the nature of her assistance was somewhat more intimate. With her skirt thrown up, legs hanging beyond the rolled edge of the desk and her corsage fully unbuttoned, she presented a picture of considerable wantonness.

Her thighs were offered above somewhat coarse brown stockings, as was her belly and thatch—a mass of dark curls from between which two rolled lips protruded. Unveiled, her breasts were of a fullness that surpassed my own in their somewhat vulgar size. Her nipples, conical and thick, were wet from the sucking they had obviously received.

I gazed entranced. Before her, with his breeches open, stood no other than Mr. Smethers, a gentleman of middle years whose fine moustache and beard were quite unable to vie for attention in that moment with the gross penis he displayed. Its erection was at its uttermost. In his hand he held a quill pen, the purpose of which escaped me for not too long. Reversing it so that its fine-pointed feather approached between her thighs, he commenced to tickle her pussy gently with it.

A rattling cry escaped her throat. Her back arched.

"OH! Oh, Mr. Smethers!"

Her large bottom worked exceedingly, spurred on by that which teased in an up and down motion between her lovelips. Her bunched-up hair, which had been tied in a bun, commenced to come awry. Her nipples strained their appeal to the ceiling.

"AH! you torture me! Oh, sir!"

"Come, Milly, will you not do it now? What a bottom-thresher you are—what hips, what thighs! Ah! have I not hungered for this!"

"You may! Ah yes, you may, sir, you may—put it in!"

He was upon her. His trousers fell to his ankles, revealing a pair of hairy, muscular legs. The rubicund crest of his charger hesitated for but a second in seeking the parting between the lips of her quim. A fluttering cry escaped her.

"Oh! it's big!"

"A size such as you deserve, Milly, and have done these past years. Ah! what succulence, what gripping!"

Lost to all but the view before me, I watched him seize her sturdy legs beneath her thighs and raise them. The motion afforded me an even more perfect view—his column being then but half embedded in her. A cry of passion broke from both. He crouched full over her, lifting her legs higher. Powerless to resist she received first his mouth and then the final stout inthrust of his tool until his big balls swung beneath her nether cheeks.

"AH!" she shrilled.

The powerful sheathing appeared to excite her tremendously. Her booted ankles wound themselves about his loins. Her heels drummed. The rather wet sounds of their kisses came to my ears.

"Woman, what a slit you have!"

"Oh, sir, sir, do it—do it—push it in!"

"My God, Milly, I shall have you daily now."

His hands sought her bottom, cupped and lifted the ripe globes. Emerging almost to the tip and gleaming with her juices, he began to pound his pestle in earnest. His balls smacked her bottom loudly. Their panting and their exchanges of lewd words became ever wilder.

I could not desist from sharing in their pleasure. My hand already had found its way up beneath my skirt. I fondled myself—I teased the moistened lips—I sought my button.

Supporting myself, I leaned one hand against the wall, half-fearful that the door might swing farther open and that I would be discovered.

'Twas in the moment that their guttural cries appeared to be reaching a peak that a hand clamped itself of a sudden over my mouth from behind. Taken utterly by surprise, I felt myself manoeuvred sideways where I fell on my knees upon an adjacent couch.

"Do not speak, or all shall be known!" a voice hissed in my ear. I hid my face in a dusty cushion, fearful to utter a sound. My skirt—already looped up by my own hand in my excitement—was thrust fully up over my hips. My naked bottom gleamed its greeting to whoever my assailant was.

A quick fumbling ensued behind me. Quiet as a fallen leaf I parted my legs in readiness. A heavy breathing sounded. A velvet-smooth knob insinuated itself precisely where I then needed it most. A hollow gasp and it had slid up. I received it, I squeezed, I pressed back. The moment was exquisite. My bottom bounced against his belly in our thrusts. Never before had I been enjoyed in such silence. From the office within sounded the moans of the two other combatants, who no doubt were reaching their crises.

I attained my own. In my pent-up state, bereaved of a penis now for several weeks, I loosed my salty spillings upon the pounding shaft of my possessor.

"Ah, little bitch!" he ground in my ear.

He thrust faster. Neither of us could contain ourselves. Had it not been for the excited sounds which reached our ears, the furtive sounds of our couplings would have betrayed us. As it was I excited him seemingly to such a pitch that in but seconds more he had loosed his sperm. I had wanted more, I had wanted longer. His jets nevertheless were considerable. The final, febrile thrusts sent more into me. Inundated I collapsed beneath him, wriggling my bottom enticingly but to no further avail.

A scuffling from within brought us quickly to our feet. I adjusted my dress. My companion was not, as I had suspected, Mr. Withers but a mere youth of some nineteen years. Seeing my face at last he looked startled, but then grinned. I sat. I could do not other. I straightened my little three-cornered hat. His look was one of supreme victory, as well it might have been. Straightening his cravat and ensuring the closure of his trousers he advanced within the office.

A scream sounded. Milly had evidently been caught with her skirt still up. The door closed. A mumbling of voices reached my ears. I made to rise and depart when the door opened anew. Mr. Smethers appeared, hastily settling his hair.

"A pleasure! I had not known you were here. Have you been waiting long?"

"A few moments, but I cannot detain myself any longer. I wish to view the property of Ashley Forest."

"Of course, of course, I will fetch the keys. You have the directions, Madam. Would you wish me to accompany you there? We have our own carriages for such purposes."

"It will not be necessary."

I measured the man with a glance. The front of his breeches showed a patch of damp.

"You have met my son? He passed into my office but a moment before."

A perfect silence as of the tomb came from within. I wondered to what extent the fallen Milly's voluptuous treasures were being examined.

"Indeed. He seems a most upcoming young man. I will convey my decision to you in a few days. Will you require a deposit?"

He bowed. "In your case, Madam, it would be entirely unnecessary. I shall hold the property upon your wish."

"Naturally. May I have the keys?"

He fumbled in his pockets as if to find them there. His front buttons not having been completely fastened, the nose of his penis showed. It peered at me with a single, enquiring eye.

"Oh, sir, that is not a key surely!"

He had the grace to blush. I affected to step back with a scream and, in doing so, nudged the door to the other office with my back. It swung open full upon its hinges. Milly was sitting in her now apparently accustomed position on the desk. Her skirt was up, her face exceedingly flushed. While Master Smethers foraged between her thighs she was bent forward dandling his prick.

I raised my hands to my cheeks as if in astonishment. Pretending equal startlement, Mr. Smethers prodded me from behind. I fell within with a screech, so seizing Milly's shoulders in the process that she fell back flat upon the desk.

"Oh, sir, you assault me! Is this how you permit your employees to behave."

Aghast they stood there—a perfect comic tableau. The re-erection of Master Smethers' penis was already in being. It had risen so far to half-size.

"What is to do! Cyril! Miss Smith! how dare you!"

His cry of hypocrisy was so obnoxious that I almost laughed.

"Do you not punish women as lewd as this? Hand me that ruler!"

Endeavouring to scramble his breeches up, young Cyril obeyed. It was two feet long and would serve my purpose admirably. In a trice, at my command, Milly was turned about, her large bottom bulging up over the edge of the desk.

THWACK! THWACK! THWACK!

I dealt the blows not too unkindly upon her nether cheeks, yet sufficiently for her to feel the sting of them. She screeched loudly. Her arms flailed.

"Be still, Miss Smith! It is well deserved!"

Mr. Smethers had entered the fray. He pinned her down. I awarded her three further smacks. The impact of the ruler on those full cheeks produced a ruddy glow. Her legs kicked. She howled. In the process I noted that Mr. Smethers' knob had now emerged in splendour from his trousers. Excitement of the spectacle had overcome him, as indeed it had young Cyril. Both were at full stand.

I profited not from it, despite my inclinations.

"What horrors you all are!"

My protestation would suffice, I believe, to deny sufficiently whatever Cyril might tell his father later. It would be taken as mere boasting. Whether his ears would now be clipped or Milly would be the panting subject of a double assault, I did not wait to see.

Closing the door upon them I waited but a moment. An expected cry reached my ears.

"Come, Cyril, lock the door! Hold her!"

"Oh, sir, no! Not both of you! OH!"

I sought the drawers of the desk close by me. Amid a bundle of keys I found those with the address I sought attached.

"OOOH, sir! Not in there!"

Milly was receiving her full due.

15

"IT IS truly delightful, Eveline. Your taste is impeccable. The view is splendid, the surroundings quiet."

"Did I not tell you so, Papa? The bedrooms are perfectly placed. No sound can be heard from one to another. And what think you of this little drawing room?"

"The acme of cosiness, my pet, but who is to protect you if you find yourself on your own?"

"I have engaged a man, Papa, a sturdy fellow. He will see to the fences, the grounds, and suchlike. There is a small lodge nearby for him. Alice will stay with me. I shall acquire one or two others to serve. Have you enjoyed Alice's company?"

He had the grace to blush. It was not my custom to enquire into his indiscretions.

"She is a frisky little thing, though still a trifle shy."

"Oh, we will cure her of that, Papa. Come, accompany me to my little bedroom, I wish to change."

Alice was in conversation on the grounds with the fellow, Lurkins, whom I had employed. He was of brawny stature and good strength. His manner was sufficiently servile to please me, but the pleasures of my face and form had obviously not escaped his eyes.

"Help me with my buttons, Papa."

"The dress is too tight, my dear, but at least you are not corseted beneath."

The trembling of his hands displayed his pleasure as I was stripped. Naked save for my stockings and shoes, I leapt from his arms. His lips would have smothered me everywhere.

"No, Papa, wait—I have a surprise for you."

Taking my tiny corset and long boots from a wardrobe, I seated myself and drew all on. Barely able to contain himself in the raising of my legs which betrayed the pouting of my nether lips, he gazed entranced as I rose at last and displayed myself to his haggard eyes.

"Ah, my goddess! Eveline, I have never seen you look so seductive!"

I was in his arms. His hands were everywhere. Our lips met in a kiss of unashamed passion.

"Enjoy your goddess, Papa. Her altar of desire awaits you. Come, strip—let us be as Lot and his daughters!"

In a moment he was naked. The sinewy muscularity of his form was mine again to enjoy. He quivered with pleasure as we stood for a long moment. My nipples tickled his chest. The suave rubbing of my leather thigh boots against his flesh maddened him.

We lay together. His hands played over me in a rapture of freedom. I raised my booted knee between his thighs. The kid leather caressed his balls. My fingers encircled his upstanding vigour, my nipples engaged his lips. Sighs of supreme pleasure escaped us.

"Do you remember you put your finger in my bottom, Papa?"

"My dear, I meant not to hurt you."

"Foolish one, it was quite enchanting. Do you think this naughty thing would fit there, too, or is it too big?"

"Ah, you witch, would you like to try it?"

For reply I turned about. His cock was at full stand. I presented him with the cheeks of my bottom. He dared to press forward so that I could no longer move. His penis quivered upright against the groove.

"Oh, Papa, it might hurt me! Perhaps we should not!"

So saying I ground my cheeks against him as if to deny the very pleasure I was inviting. Exactly as I hoped a growl of uttermost desire broke from him. His hand seized the nape of my neck, forcing my face down further into the pillow.

I whined, I murmured. I felt the valley parting as the knob intruded. Resistance would inflame him all the more, I knew. I twisted, I choked, I sobbed.

"Please don't, Papa!"

My hypocrisy was, I believe, apparent to him. His grip on my neck lightened as if to permit me to rise if I wanted. Instead I twisted my face from side to side. My rose yielded. The rubbery rim gave to the probing it sustained.

"It is too wicked, Papa! Oh, stop!"

"I shall have it, Eveline—I have long dreamed of this!

Your bottom is perfection! What marble surfaces, what inviting warmth! Ah! it is IN!"

I moaned. I yielded by degrees. I trembled in every limb as he bore slowly within. Seizing my chin he brought my face about and crouched further over me. Our tongues entwined like the necks of doves as I adjusted myself to the greater part of his virility. Every inch of its sheathing was an electric thrill. A cloud of pleasure fogged my mind. I uttered incoherent cries. Conscious of nothing but the delicious sensation as he finally corked me to the full, I began to further his endeavours by rotating my hips lewdly.

In such moments the body becomes like a fine violin to be played upon with infinite care and skill. A good melody is never rushed. The vibrant elasticity of my youthful form, coupled with the patience our mutual endeavours brought to the occasion, ensured the increasing throbbings of pleasure in both our loins.

"Do you like it, Eveline? Oh, my lovely daughter, I am in your bottom at last. What bliss!"

Indeed he was. I had him to the full. His balls urged against my slit. Bringing my hand beneath me I swirled my forefinger about my button.

"Move it slowly, Papa—your Eveline has never had it before. How big you feel in there—how you throb! Ah, what wickedness, what excesses! Let me feel it—push the whole length in again!"

I shuddered, I moaned, I rocked. The movement between us became easier. I had lubricated his cock a little by perspiring within. His groans were exceeding. I bit the pillow in my ecstasy.

"Do not come too soon, Papa—your Eveline wants to feel it all!"

In withdrawing, his knob all but slipped from the rim. The renewed upward thrust caused me to spill in sweet agony upon my working finger. Papa knelt upright. His hands held my hips but lightly. I jerked them back and forth, assisting the oozing piston. My senses swam. I encouraged the longer, faster thrusts I now received. A divine shudder passed between us as our rhythmical efforts encouraged the inevitable climax.

"Oh, Papa! I am coming again! Have me! Take me! Remember whose bottom you have it in!"

"My darling, AH! How you wriggle it! What joy!"

"Pump faster, Papa, you are coming—I can feel it!"

Indeed I could. The long warm jets entered my bottom as fiercely as a cannonade. His cries were frantic. Thrusting in me to the full and gripping my hips in his strong hands he loosed his load with a vigour I had never known before. From the abundance of his libation it was evident that his pleasure was doubled by this unconventional route.

We flopped sideways at last. I held it within me. I felt its diminishing, though the process was luxuriously slow. His hands cupped my breasts, his thumbs toyed with my nipples. Sensations of untold bliss quivered through us still. I turned my face at last. Our lips met in tenderness. I wriggled the hot cheeks of my bottom mischievously upon him.

"What pleasures you teach me, Papa."

My tongue licked his own. The sensuousness of all that had passed knew no hypocrisy. From the first moments of our incestuous *ébats* long months before, we had made no pretence about our flouting of Society.

"I shall have it again, Eveline—you promise me?"

"I deny you nothing, Papa. You shall have your Eveline as you want. You have taught me all. You have had my nether virginity now. Oh! it is in me still! Can you? Can you again, Papa?"

He needed no further bidding. The lustfulness of our

desires had long been exchanged. I pressed myself further down, engaging the thick worm tightly. The silken cheeks of my bottom bulged to him. The backs of my soft boots pressed against the fronts of his thighs. I felt him stiffen anew. The sensation reached right down to my toes. I whispered such obscenities as he longed to hear. In our newly arising lust we exchanged the coarsest of words.

"Sperm your daughter, Papa—let her feel it."

Without disengaging his cock which now filled me again, he rolled me upon my knees. I offered myself up. My moans of desire rang in my pillow. The bedsprings sang their song. We were as one, rising to the very summits of desire.

"Alice, will you like it here?"

"Oh yes, Miss, I loves the country. The air is fresher and the folks nicer."

"How do you get on with Lurkins? You must both protect me now that Lord L. is gone."

"We shall both do that, Miss. He will not sleep at nights, I'm sure, but he has set traps around for any villains that may try and enter."

"I am pleased to hear it, Alice. I must go and talk to him."

Lurkins was lurking, as was his wont. I walked across to the stables where he loitered.

"You have seen Lord L. off?"

"Yes, Missy. He said as he was going on to Eastbourne and that you might join him there."

I nodded. Papa would have said nothing of the sort to such a lowly fellow. No doubt Lurkins had overheard Papa's instructions to the coachman.

"What are you doing now, Lurkins?"

"Piling up some hay, Missy, in here."

He motioned to the gloom within. I peered. I went forward. He followed me.

"It is a good pile, Lurkins. You must be very strong to have lifted all that."

"I am that, Missy. There's none around here who would defy me. I am built strong all over."

He gestured rather crudely. I leaned back against a bale of straw.

"ALL over, Lurkins? I would need some proof of that."

He peered behind him somewhat furtively. There was clearly no one else about.

"With permission, Missy, I'll show you. They say it's the biggest for many a mile around. See—it's got stiff already with the warmth of the day and the rubbing against my breeches."

It was indeed a monster. The veins stood proud upon it. Emerging, it stiffened to full size. A donkey was scarcely hung better.

"What do you do with it, Lurkins?"

The invitation was sufficient. I was spun about. His rude hands hesitated not. My skirt was flung up. The sight of my nudity beneath brought a gasp of pleasure.

"Bend over and open your legs wider, Missy, and I'll show you!"

"It will never go in, Lurkins—it's too big. OH! Not so fast! Do you do all the girls this way?"

"Everyone in the village, Missy, what wears a skirt, young and old—they're raring keen for it. How tight you are—I can scarce get it in!"

"Oh, wait, you are splitting me! Let me bend over more, there. Now try! Ah, what a monster it is. Push slowly! OOOOH!"

I measured it bigger than John's. The lips of my quim

gaped about it. Three-quarters of it had engaged me. I felt the breath expelled from my lips. His hands groped for my breasts. I thrust them away.

"No! just do it!"

"I loves a good fuck, Missy, don't you? Move your bottom back! What whiteness, what curves! Lovely legs you got—open 'em wider! Do you like it?"

I could scarce speak. But half an hour before I had risen from the bed with Papa, twice anointed in my most secret place. Now I was receiving a Samson by the more conventional route.

"Not all of it, Lurkins! OH!"

Too late—the fellow had oozed right in. The fact that I could contain it all astonished me. He throbbed madly in my tight, silk purse. Every pulsing of his veins was conveyed to me. His fingers were greedy about my thighs.

"Stop it, Lurkins! You may service me, that is all! Push now—faster!"

He groaned his pleasure. My grip was exceedingly tight, though lubricated already by my little orgy with Papa. The word "service" had come to me of a sudden. He appeared to understand it, no doubt from his farmyard work. His loins thrust lustily. I came in a spurting of joy, though I conveyed it not to him. His emission would be considerable, I knew. Bending his knees he pressed them into the backs of mine. I was as dove beneath the ox. He snorted, he thrust.

"Oh, Missy, I want to come!"

"Do it, Lurkins, I want to feel it."

I threshed my bottom. The elasticity of my vagina held him to the full. His balls, smacking beneath me, were surely as big as a bull's. I felt his quivers. The first onrush was nigh.

"A good fuck, Missy, a good fuck—WHOOOOOO!"

Huge pellets of sperm followed by thick strings of his

glutinous outpouring spattered and filled me. Pumping out mightily, his sperm ran down over his huge tool, easing its passage until his loins literally flashed.

"Ah, Missy, I never come so much!"

I did not doubt it. He had never had so shapely and luring a filly to mount. I stilled my transports. I enjoyed his cries. The itching thrusts of his cock, swimming in our mingling juices, would in other circumstances have caused me to cry out with pleasure. I desisted. Such a fellow did not deserve my attentions in that manner. When he withdrew at last I remarked to myself upon the way in which I had changed. Henceforth I would share my transports only with such as I chose to. Bullocks such as Lurkins would be put to servicing.

I felt the slipping out of his cock at last. I rose. I fixed my hair. I obtained composure. The greasy pole still looked of worthy size even though hanging limp.

"That will do, Lurkins. Get on with your work now."

"Yes, Missy."

He had not met my like before. His look was one of doleful wonder. I brushed passed him, avoiding with my skirt the slight dripping of his tool. Sperm fell in little drops down my thighs. The luxury of the sensation was ever pleasant. Without according him a further glance I returned to the cottage.

Alice was a picture of innocence.

"Has Lord L. been nice to you, Alice?"

"Oh yes, Miss."

Her blush could not be concealed. Her purse had profited much therefrom, I guessed.

"Be careful of that fellow, Lurkins, Alice. He is a worthy worker, but he has a certain look about him."

"Oh I will, Miss. He's attempted me already. I wouldn't have none of it."

"You are a good girl, Alice. Tell him to have the carriage out in an hour. I want to drive to Lewes."

I took lunch. Alice was an able enough little cook, but I would have to have a woman to prepare better collations for Papa and others. Lurkins waited with the horse when I had finished. Entering the main roadway we halted as another carriage passed. A face stared at me from within.

It was the fellow who had assaulted me in the railway carriage.

16

*L*EWES is an ancient town, possessed of the ruins of a fine castle set high on a hill. I visited it. I am fond of old places. They breathe of events long passed, of riots, revels, war and peace, and lovemaking—of lusts long scattered in the dust.

A shadow fell over my own as I gazed beyond the battlements. A quiver of anticipation ran through me. I turned slowly. It was he.

"I feared to approach you yet I could not help it. My conscience has ever worried me."

"Your conscience or the state of your purse, sir?"

His visage fell even more. His hand waved.

"My purse? 'Tis as nothing to my honour. I swear I had never thus assaulted a lady before. Your prettiness, your beauty, quite overcame me. What recompense can I ever give you?"

"The reply, sir, is not in my hands, for I know you not. Clearly you are one of those rogues who believe that any woman's skirts may be lifted freely. My poor maid was terrified."

"Yet you fondled and kissed her!"

Emboldened by the fact that I had not screamed nor run from him in front of the several other people nearby, his impertinence was great. I moved past him, my head high.

"How dare you speak to me like that? Who are you?"

"Lord Wilkins, m'am—and forever at your service. At least I do beg such a lowly station. My tongue forever runs ahead of me."

"Not only your tongue, sir. You had more than that sticking out on the last occasion that we met."

I endeavoured to hide a smile. I was unable to.

"You live here? Have I discovered your domicile at last? I have never ceased to think of you since that dreadful incident."

"I am visiting only. I am pleased at your description, at least. It was truly dreadful. Do you intend following me like this?"

"Solely as your protector. Lewes is a quiet enough place, but one never knows."

"I trust you are not staying here also."

"I am indeed." He named an hotel. I quickly named another for myself that I had noticed in passing. Both were in the High Street. I did not intend any but the most favoured—if ever such there were—to know where I stayed. Beseeching the kindness of a few words of forgiveness from me, he continued to follow.

"Very well—you may buy me a glass of wine at your hotel, but no more."

His joy was plain. We crossed amid the passing vehicles and entered. He was on business about the district, it appeared, buying up agricultural land. Fortunately the places he mentioned lay well south of my cottage. A bottle of wine was soon dispensed with.

"Will you not come to my room for a moment? I cannot make amends here."

I protested that it was an unseemly suggestion. I knew full well the implement he intended to make amends with. In the end I appeared to soften. An uncertain lift propelled us upwards. In the corridor we entered a rather pretty maid passed us.

"She is an attractive girl."

"Indeed she is. She sees to my room. I am pleased to learn that you have a liking for other women. Was that why you were feeling your maid's thighs in the carriage."

"Perhaps."

We were already in his room. He drew my mouth to his. There are moments when dissimulation is unnecessary.

"Shall I call her for you?"

The direct invitation surprised me.

"Has she not a housekeeper who will miss her?"

"She is easily bribed. It will take but a moment."

"Wait! What are you at?"

"To see two attractive young women pleasuring one another is an enjoyment I would never miss."

"While you enjoy the one who is upon the other?"

"You will permit it?"

I laughed. "I will make sure she is uppermost, then. Have her lustily, for I enjoy watching."

The truth was out between us. I intended him not to see me again in any event. Lurkins would be long in waiting for me to rejoin my carriage, but he must learn to muster the same patience as Jim had always done.

In five minutes Lord Wilkins had returned with the girl. She wore a shy look. She stood mute. He laid a ten pound note upon the dressing table.

"You may pick it up after you have undressed, Kate."

"Oh, sir—but the lady!"

I laid another note upon his own. Her eyes were like saucers. I lay back upon the bed and drew my gown up. My thighs and all above my stocking tops came into view. I parted my thighs. His gaze grew feverish. Without ado he commenced unbuttoning the back of her dress. Kate moved and blushed. He drew her skirts up, displaying a finely curved pair of legs. Wearing no drawers, she displayed a thick bush.

"Uncover her breasts. Let me see them. Bring her to me."

"Is he your husband, Madam?"

She gasped as she was flung upon me. I had meanwhile uncovered my own breasts. They bulbed sweetly beneath her own.

"No, he is my uncle."

"Oh, Madam!"

My legs coiled up about her waist. I held her tight. The wide parting of my thighs allowed our slits to kiss. I drew her blazing cheeks down to mine and sought her mouth. I whispered. I intruded my tongue. Her lips were soft and sweet. I drew her skirt higher by groping down her back. Her bottom reared to him.

"He fucks me frequently. My aunt watches. We have lovely times. Come, give me your tongue, his cock is ready for you."

"OH!" She would have reared and twisted if I had not

gripped her tightly with my calves while simultaneously Lord Wilkins knelt behind her, his penis in as ready a condition as it would ever be.

"I don't want to!"

She began to whine and sob. Her cries were interspersed with breathless gasps as he slowly invaded her. I doubted not that her passage was sweet and tight. I held her, cradled her. His cock worked its will. In a moment her lax lips returned to mine. Her pleasure bubbled out in little muffled cries such as I loved to hear.

"Work your hips, Kate—let him have you! Isn't it nice? Don't you like having a big cock?"

"Oh, it's so wicked!"

The thrills she was receiving between us were now unconcealed. Her nipples sprung starkly against my own. Gliding my hand down between us I found her button. She began to twist deliriously. Such sophistication would never have entered her mind before. Our tongues worked faster. I felt her spray, her spillings. Though of slender build like myself, she was lusty enough for any man once she had been awoken.

"F . . . f . . . faster! Oh, sir, Oh, madam!"

"You naughty girl—push back and forth. Give it to him!"

"Oh, I want to, yes! Oh! Oh! I never had it like this before!"

The bed trembled. If anyone was in the bedroom below they might have feared a collapse of the ceiling. We jolted, we gasped, the throes of pleasure overtook us. The sound of her bottom cheeks slapping against his belly rose above all.

"Ah, the lovely little creature, I am coming in her!"

"Madam! Oh! He is doing it! AH!"

Coaxed and fondled she lay between us. Lord Wilkins appeared to accept that I was ordaining events. Sandwiching her between us I fondled his prick with my arm lying upon her hip. The state of being half undressed pleased me. I fondled her thighs. I sucked her tongue.

"I must go, Madam, in a minute. They'll be missing me."

"No, Kate, you will do as you are told."

I toyed with her quim. She was in a veritably creamy state. I rubbed the stickiness over the tops of her stockings and around the smooth warm flesh of her thighs. Her mouth lolled open more. She accepted my tongue. Her own played prettily. Tightly packed together as we were she murmured frettingly as her bottom was feted by his hands. The hot rubbing of her cheeks was bringing his revival. I felt behind her. The stiff column of flesh was pressed tight against her groove.

I held her shoulders. Leaning my weight upon her I bent over and kissed him. I toyed with the conjunction of their flesh.

"Have her bottom. I want to see it!"

"No! Oh, Madam, no!"

She endeavoured to sit up. Laughing he held her down. I swung my leg over her so that she was imprisoned.

"Is there a strap? Fetch it!"

He was off the bed in a flash. The implement for wayward young misses was evidently not unknown to him. Grinning hugely and with cock bobbing erect he flourished one that had fastened around a travelling trunk.

"Madam! don't let him!"

Her cries, her wails, were of no avail. Despite the strength she showed I succeeded in rolling her over. I rose. I placed one knee firmly in her back. Her cries muffled themselves in a pillow as the broad leather descended upon her quivering buttocks with a loud THWACK!

"Six! She will obey then!"

Her hips heaved. Endeavouring madly to escape the burning salute, she succeeded in having her bottom only further striped. It assumed a fine, rosy hue. The satiny skin looked well polished.

THWACK! SMACK! THWACK!

To each one her belly bounced anew. I could scarce contain my posture. My stockinged knee drummed on her back.

"Oh! stop him! I won't let him. NO!"

"Six more and then she will. Give it to her!"

"Yes, all right, I will! Oh, it burns, it burns!"

"Nonsense! It has but prepared you for the fray, Kate. Lift your bottom or it will get truly scorched. Come on, now!"

Despite a slight lifting of her hips, accompanied by a wild weaving of the bottom which the strap had now caressed eight times, her mutinous behaviour was clear. I gave her a sharp smack on the buttocks with my palm. She yelped.

"Kate! lift it! No nonsense now."

Quivering and sobbing she obeyed, her face full hidden in her hands. Tears pearled between her fingers. I would have felt sorry for her if I had not known the sensations that were about to pleasure her. Clambering once more upon the bed, his cock was presented. Kate jerked. I held her wrist.

"Slowly now—I wish her to enjoy it."

"I won't, I won't, it's too big! It can't go up there!"

Her protests were ignored. The rim of her rosette succumbed as I knew it must to the gentle pressure he applied. Drawing her hips back he entered it slowly, his face a picture to see. Her bottom was fulsome enough and must have been according him the utmost pleasure. His grimaces told everything.

"AH! NO! AH!"

She began to buck like a kicking mule, or would have done if between us we had not quelled her movements. The cork was but three inches in. His enraptured gaze caught mine. I nodded. Opened now as she was she could well receive the rest. The splitting of her globe by his prick enchanted me. Powerful as a piston of a railway engine it urged within. Kate's head jerked up once and then fell. Her back hollowed, her bottom presenting a perfect peach.

"Oh my God, how tight she is! I am in!"

"T . . . t . . . take it out! OH! it hurts!"

I stroked her hair. The loveliness of her form was evident in the supple curving she presented to his will with a secretly greater eagerness than she uttered. Breath puffed from her lips in a small explosion as his cock was majestically withdrawn almost to the crest and then entered again.

I released my own hold upon her. The fluttering of her eyelashes told me all. A savagery of pleasure was about to overtake her. Her bottom was unable to resist a questing push as if she could not believe she could contain it all.

"Good, Kate—now move it slowly."

My voice came to her in a whisper. I parted her tousled hair. I anointed her cheeks with my lips. In a moment by turning her face more the tips of our tongues touched.

"Is it nice, Kate? Do you like it now?"

Her eyes rolled upwards in her head. I knew her condition. The pestle was moving more easily now in the pot. Her natural lubrications had eased it. Despite the commanding manner in which I had put her to this I intended her pleasure. My finger sought her clitoris. Her cries bubbled. Confused by the thrills she was unexpectedly obtaining she began to thrust her tongue with long strokes into my mouth.

Lord Wilkins panted, he puffed. He would be longer about it than he had been in her vagina, I knew. The thick stem of his cock emerged and thrust within again and again.

I felt her throbbings, the pulsings of her nest. Blabbering incoherently she flung one arm awkwardly about my neck. I slid down. I manoeuvred my face beneath her own.

"Do you want it, Kate?"

"Oh yes, yes—YES—AAAAH!"

His come was long in its jerkings. Her own tribute flourished wetly with it. Panting, she lay supine when at last he had uncorked.

"Make sure he gives you the money. Do not let him cheat you, Kate."

"Oh, Madam, you are not leaving!"

"I must, Kate."

I had but to throw down my skirt, ruffled as it was and button my front. Lord Wilkins immediately got off the bed where he had perhaps expected my own surrender. His hushed whisper came to my ear.

"I shall see you again? I do not even know your name!"

"I pass through here occasionally—or we may meet perhaps in London. Be careful that someone in the corridor does not see you in your condition!"

He made to place his hand upon the door but I had already opened it.

"Be sure that you give her all of the twenty pounds. I shall enquire of her later. She has earned it gallantly."

I passed beyond, flattering myself that Kate had learned several lessons that could not but benefit her in the future. Several weeks later when I ventured into Lewes again—Lord Wilkins having told me that he had but a few days to stay there—I encountered Kate dressed in much finery parading in the High Street. In no doubt as to what she was at, I accosted her.

"Oh, Madam, I did not expect to see you again!"

I drew her into a nearby coffee shop.

"What are you at, Kate?"

Her expression fell. It was obvious to her that she had incurred my displeasure. Her halting account of how she had left the hotel and gone upon the streets was quickly interrupted.

"I will not have it, Kate. You are a fool! Never display your wares so openly. The hotel offers you fine shelter and food, does it not? Give at all times an impression of propriety, of demureness. The rewards will be all the greater. There are many gentlemen who will entertain you on the quiet. Affect always to be a model of purity until you are within the bedroom. Good heavens, Lewes is such a small town you are making a spectacle of yourself!"

She began to snivel. Yes it was true, she said. A policeman had already warned her. She could not take a job again in Lewes. They all knew about her.

"Then you will go to Eastbourne, Kate. I know the proprietors of several well-to-do establishments there. I will give you a note. You will secure a post easily. You will write me and let me know that you are settled. Here is my London address."

She gazed at me in awe. My words of wisdom had sunk home.

"I will do as you say, yes, Madam. I know you are right. I will look nice and proper, as you say, and it will benefit me better."

I gave her a further guinea to ensure her passage. She had spent almost all the twenty pounds on her vulgar attire and her rooms. I helped her gather such few belongings as she had and saw her aboard a coach.

"I'll never know how to thank you, Madam. I haven't seen your uncle again." Her eyes regarded me curiously. After my little speech she did not know what to make of me.

"I do not see him often, Kate. He became a bore. All men

do. You will discover that for yourself soon enough. No woman need prostitute herself on the streets if she knows how to behave."

A wave and she was gone. I had saved her from a fate that would have dragged her down. When I next saw her again in Eastbourne she told me that she was a chambermaid again and that her jewellery box already contained a number of nice pieces.

17

"THE Vicar to see you, Miss."

Alice entered the drawing room all a-flutter. I motioned to her to show him in. The hour was early for visitors, but I understood that some clerics were tireless in their workings.

He who was presented to me was younger than I expected, a ruddy-cheeked young man who looked as well-polished as a cherub. I offered him a glass of wine. Those of the church were often great imbibers, Papa had once told me. The Reverend Nobb's surprise to find me living alone was evident. I assured him of protectors.

"I trust I shall have the pleasure of seeing you in church soon, Miss Eveline."

"That may be so. I am not given to prostrating myself publically behind a pew, however. Do you not sometimes feel that Nature itself has its own fine spirit? I am a life-worshipper, a sun-worshipper, you know."

My reply confounded him, as it was intended to do. I arrayed myself in girlish manner upon the sofa beside him. Our glasses were replenished.

"Life indeed is to be worshipped, yes, but . . ."

"Do you live alone? Are you married?"

A slight blush pervaded his features. I had interrupted him of a purpose. I was older than he by centuries.

"I live with my mama and my sister."

"Then they are truly fortunate, Vicar. To have, I mean, someone so handsome and wise at their sides."

"How kind you are, Miss Eveline. Oh heavens, you have spilled some wine on your pretty dress—permit me!"

He produced a kerchief and commenced to mop at my thigh where I had allowed several drops to fall. My hand engaged his own in the process.

"Not there—a little higher! See—there is some in the fold of my dress. Let me lean back and you will find it better. It has quite soaked through. Can you feel?"

His expression was one to behold. In rearranging my posture I had drawn my dress up somewhat. How many pairs of female legs he had seen before I know not. Mine appeared to entrance him. He was as one transfixed. His hand encountered my bared thighs.

"What are you at? How naughty of you! Oh, it tickles, but it is nice! Pray continue for I am almost converted!"

The absence of drawers gave him much to see. He appeared mesmerised, for my movement had brought his fingers in intimate contact with my vagina. An uprising appeared in the lower half of his cassock. I clutched it. A look of wonderment appeared in his eyes.

"Oh, Miss Eveline!"

"Oh, Vicar!"

I sought beneath the folds of his attire. A fleshy rod burned its greeting to my palm. I enfolded it in my clasp. An air of entrancement entered my features. The sweetness of my mouth could not but attract him. The sliver of tongue which I presented to his must have made his senses boil.

"What a large one! Is this how I must embrace the church?"

A veritable ague seized him. The open lolling of my legs was a clear invitation.

"AH! I want to!"

The exclamation escaped him as he fell upon me. I guided the knob of the Reverend Nobb to its haven. The curls about my slit tickled the plum.

"Oh! what a steeple you have! How rigid, how tall!"

"Forgive me, Miss Eveline, I cannot but help it. What an adorable creature you are! Alas, we are fallen into sin!"

"Put it in, then, or the Devil may get it! Not so quick! OH! a little more! Push it up!"

The sofa trembled, though no more than he. I had him all but fully ensconced. The sceptre throbbed within me. The silky grip of my lovepurse engaged him fully. A single jerk, a mutual moan of pleasure, and the treasure was fully buried.

"Move it a little now! Oh, how masterful you are! I am being anointed, am I not? Is that not what you call it?"

"Indeed, yes! What a luscious grip you have! Let me feel your bottom! What perfection. Oh, I shall anoint you too soon, I fear!"

"Not yet, not yet—I want to feel it more! Do it slowly

and you will enjoy it the better. Oh! I am coming! What a lovely sensation! You are making me melt! OH!"

My last exclamation was occasioned not by the pleasure I was receiving with my naked bottom now cupped upon his hands, but by the sudden appearance of Alice. His cock but half sheathed in back and forward motions at that moment, the Vicar turned his head and was as one frozen.

"Oh, Miss!"

"Oh, Alice!"

Such things as happened then were no doubt ordained by fate. The door swung to behind her, caught by some errant breeze. The rug beneath her slipped, causing her to fall with a bump and a screech. In the process her skirt flew up. A nest sweet enough for any cockbird to enter presented itself.

"Quickly, Vicar!"

He was out of me in quite a daze, his penis bobbing a greeting to the air.

"Ah! we are undone!"

"Seize her! Bring her here!"

Floundering wildly and assisted by my more authoritative presence, Alice was drawn up and lifted to the sofa whence we had arisen in such haste. I assured that her skirt remained risen. Hair tousled, red of cheeks, Alice emitted a squeak and would have risen.

"No, Alice! How naughty you are to peep! Do you mean to tell all, Miss? Well, you shall not? Quickly, Vicar, there is but one way to ensure her silence. No doubt she needs anointing even more than I. Quickly, you fool, get upon her!"

"Miss! NO! OH!"

My urging hands accompanied by a fervent squeeze upon his penis, effected all. Maddened by the voluptuous nature of our embrace, his muscular legs quelled the struggles of her own. A breathless shriek from Alice and the fleshly piston was within.

"OOOOH! OOOH! AAAAH!"

Alice jogged and jolted, his balls pendant in salute against the chubby cheeks of her bottom. The flaming shaft was full buried in. The contractions of his buttocks were as expressive as the look of enchantment on his face.

"Ah my goodness, what a lovely one!"

A stuttering from Alice and his lips smothered her own. I slipped my fingers down beneath the conjunction of their parts and felt the oily ringing of her lovemouth about his pestle.

"Spare her not, she needs it more than I, Vicar! Oh, what a wicked sight! Do it to her quickly now, you are bound to come in a minute!"

Puffing and panting, Alice worked her bottom. The luscious sounds of belly-smacking grew. His pubic hairs rubbed and ground upon her own. Her face softened, her eyes rolled. The little minx was giving him first the benefit of her own effusion. Flashing in and out, his stiff penis gleamed with her juices.

"AH! I am coming!"

Alice's legs shot straight out, remaining curiously rigid in the air for a moment. Clearly she was at the peak of her pleasure. Bending her knees anew she lifted and tightened them about his waist.

"I can feel it! OOOH! Oh, what a lot!"

A lot indeed. His cock literally foamed. I had knelt to see all. I could not contain myself. My hand worked busily between my thighs, though neither could see. The trickles of sperm coursing back down his gristle to cream her lovelips were evidence enough of his pent-up powers. A giant shudder and he collapsed, all but burying Alice beneath him.

"A brandy, Vicar. You must recuperate your strength."

"What have I done? Oh woe, what have I done!"

"Fret not, you have but exercised the staff of life. We frail females are destined to receive its glorious essence. It must ever be. Come, drink, you will feel all the better for it. Alice—do you feel a sinner?"

"No, Miss, I liked it. It were nice. I felt it were the same as going to church only better."

"How kind you both are! Oh, blessed am I to have been received among angels!"

The brandy gurgled down his throat. His Adam's apple worked its pleasure. With his cassock thrown open and my own and Alice's thighs bared still we presented a picture of heavenly wantonness. My hand cupped his balls. Her own dandled his penis.

"You must exercise it more, Vicar. The poor thing has been quite neglected, has it not? It needs as good a run every day as your dogs and horses do. Alice, give it a little suck, for I am sure it is but waiting to perk up its head again."

A groan of rapture escaped him. Tutored as she had undoubtedly been in Papa's bed whence I had first sent her, Alice's cupid mouth enclosed the plum within. Truly he must have thought himself in heaven. I continued to caress his balls. We exchanged the least pure of kisses. I spread my legs that his hand might fondle my dell.

"It is I who was robbed of your essence, Vicar."

"N . . . n . . . not for long, I trust! Oh my goodness, what a lovely feeling! She is bringing it up again!"

I looked down. A fever of excitement was evident in all three of us. The ministrations of Alice's lips had brought him rapidly up to a fine stand again.

"Let me, Alice! I want to take the saddle!"

Seated as he was, she fell back laughing. I swung myself

upon him, face to face. The luring of my eyes and mouth could no more be denied than the downward pressure of my lovelips upon his bulbous knob. A sigh of ecstasy and it entered. My knees gripped his hips. My bottom began its sleek up and down movements. Of a sudden, seized by a lewdness, I slid my hands down behind me and parted the cheeks of my bottom.

"Put your tongue there, Alice!"

She obeyed, crouched beneath me. Curling like a leaf, the tip of her tongue tickled my rosehole deliciously. I would later learn that the French designated this caress *"feuille de rose."* A trilling of pleasure escaped my throat. I moved more slowly, the better to receive the double salute. The Vicar panted and groaned, making little febrile movements of his hips. I had all in control. I pumped at will.

"Put it in, Alice! A little more! OOOH!"

Our gasps resounded. Poor Alice, twisted beneath me and propped upon one elbow, had her nose frequently bumped by the agitations of my bottom. Valiantly she continued her wicked task. Her tongue licked everywhere.

"AH! I cannot hold it back!"

"Come in me, come! I am doing it too!"

My bottom descended full upon his thighs. Sheathed to the root within me his penis pulsed its leaps while Alice in her acrobatics continued to make my hips writhe and jerk.

Finally all was expended. I fell sideways. I dismounted. My eyes were dimmed with pleasure. As for Vicar, he must have counted himself a convert rather than a preacher. Restoring all order in due course he took his leave of me. I escorted him outside to where his horse stood reined to a fence. He appeared a trifle dazed. His whole world, I suspected, had been turned upside down. I made merry of his discomposure.

"You will call again, I trust? We have imbibed much that was good."

"You mean it, Miss Eveline? I would fear to disturb you again after my untoward behaviour."

He assumed the doleful look of one who hopes to be contradicted.

"What nonsense! It would be indeed a drab world if people did not get carried away sometimes. You just come to tea. Bring your sister."

"My sister? Would it not distract from our—er—communion?"

"Perhaps not. It might add to it!"

I gave his horse a slap. It went off at a trot. Twisting about, his bemused glance followed me as I went back into the cottage.

18

I ATTAINED my majority. The magical age of twenty-one was upon me. The weather growing dull, I left the cottage to the care of Lurkins and a new cook of matronly and reliable aspect. I returned with Alice to London. Her conversion was complete. I could rely on her discretion.

"The Vicar's sister, Miss! Oh, what a rare lark that were!"

"A spinster in mind and body she would have remained otherwise, Alice. Truly we have done her a service. What wonders a few glasses of port and convivial company will do! How she bumped and squealed at first!"

"Fair raring for a little cuddling, she were, though. How did you say he had her, Miss?"

"Via the crypt rather than the chapel, Alice! I guessed he might—a fair bottom she has for it. Clerics are said to be given more to such pleasures, as I have often been told. Once in, he had her, though. I don't think she believed it was happening at first, what with the tickling and the laughter that went on."

"Until you rolled her over and gave her bottom a smack. Oh, he was into her then quick enough!"

"And made a good bout of it, Alice. People should never deny themselves, though in truth I never thought to see such a thing. Her snivelling afterwards did her for little. It took not much persuasion to have her entertain him a second time. The poor thing will be quite put out if she is not able to keep him up to it now—on the quiet."

"Oh yes, Miss, that's always best 'cept when you're in the know with others, ain't it."

I did not answer. My sudden silences helped to keep her in awe of me. Impetuous as I sometimes appeared to her, I could also be stern. In giving her to understand that she shared all my secrets, I kept the most important from her.

"Shall you not have a ball, Eveline, to celebrate your coming of age?"

"Perhaps, Papa, but I want to think carefully upon the list of guests we invite. A small, discreet gathering would be better than a large one, do you not think?"

"It shall be ever as my little girl wishes. Do you think to marry again? In a few months time it would be proper to consider the matter."

"Oh? You wish to marry me off? No, dearest Papa, that was but said in joke. In truth I cannot bear to think of myself again bound to one man day and night. A bedroom regularly shared is an opportunity frequently lost. Let us continue rather to disport ourselves as we do at present and to value our freedom above all other. Do you think me cold of heart for saying that?"

"You are warm in every aspect, my pet. I would have it no other way. I merely wish not to hinder your progress."

"Dearest Papa, you will never do that. In a few years' time, perhaps when I am twenty-five, I may reconsider the matter. Meanwhile both London and the countryside bore me. Shall we away? I have seen little enough of Paris. They say it is a most wicked city."

"What a splendid idea, Eveline! I will arrange our passage immediately. Be sure to bring your thigh boots and your adorable waist corsets."

"Of course. How soon may we depart, d'you think?"

"In but two days, my love. Shall we not have a little rehearsal now?"

"No, you must wait, for then you will be even more desirous and I infinitely more wicked. Be sure that we pass under names other than our own when we reach our hotel, or complications may ensue. Besides, we shall have more freedom in our adventures in that way."

He would have seized me in my laughter had we not been interrupted. John announced a visitor. It was the Police Inspector.

"I will see him in the drawing room, John. We must not be interrupted."

"What is it, Eveline? Has there been trouble?"

"Not at all, Papa. A small case of theft which I witnessed. No doubt the fellow wants to take a statement from me."

I attended upon the man. His look, though grave, was avid. John closed the door. I locked it.

"What is it, Inspector?"

"The matter of that photographer, Miss. Witnesses is needed. I am trying to keep your name out of it."

"As well you must. I see no difficulty about that."

"None as would be except for the little girl in it what has hopped off. A few words from her—or yourself—would have given them villains another couple of years."

"You have an abundance of plates, Inspector, that speak for themselves. I want no more of it. Surely you can devise sufficient evidence?"

"It's the Judge, Miss. He's very enquiring—seeks out all the nooks and corners as you might say. I has a proper job with him."

"Concern yourself not, Inspector—I know means of avoiding any catastrophe. It would not do for the Judge to know how the Inspector at Scotland Yard disported himself with certain witnesses, would it? Leave all to me. I will speak to Sir Langham Beamish. He will settle it."

The fellow's face fell. His eyes were all about my figure. I knew his game. I did not intend to sport with him in the house in order that he might then pretend to be able to cover up my identity. He dared not reveal it or his career would be at stake.

"That will be all, Inspector."

"Yes, Miss. I thought only to give help where it was due."

I unlocked the door. In other circumstances I might have let him have his will but my thoughts now were rather on Paris. I intended to pleasure myself as never before.

"To Paris, Miss? Cor, I would love to come!"

"No, Alice, I'm afraid not, but you may help me pack.

Together I fear that we might fall into indiscretions. You know how severe Lord L. is in such matters."

Her expression fell. She thought me a great innocent in all matters to do with Papa and herself. I did not intend disillusioning her. This particular facade was one I intended always to maintain.

The crossing was smooth. By nightfall on the following Friday we had reached Paris. The Champs Élysées glittered with its fairy lights. The cuisine at the hotel on the Rue St. Georges was superb. I wore a gown of white that glittered with sequins. My stockings and shoes matched.

"How sweet and virginal you look, Eveline. Few would take you even for twenty-one!"

"I mean it so to be, Papa. The *midinettes* in the streets appear wanton enough with their wriggling bottoms and sidelong glances. An appearance of purity will assist us. Think how many times you may have me seduced, if you wish!"

Papa laughed. His hand laid itself upon my thigh beneath the damask table cloth. The warmth of my flesh was as an intoxicant to him. We had entered ourselves in the hotel register as Major and Miss Brown. No one would ever learn our identities. The city of sin would cover us with anonymity. Our bedrooms adjoined, but were separate.

"I know just what would suit you, my love. There is a certain club I have heard of. It encloses a private erotic theatre such as the nobility in the grand days of Versailles were said to enjoy. The walls hang with the most lewd paintings that once adorned the boudoir of Madame Pompadour." [Editor's Note: This little sidepiece of history is undoubtedly correct. Reproductions of some of the paintings in the collection of that wanton aristocrat have since been widely dispersed in reproduction. One such, attributed to the painter Boucher, shows a pretty young woman with one leg poised upon a chair, presenting her bare bottom. Behind her a man is in the act of inserting his penis in her. All details are finely delineated.]

"How splendid, Papa! Can we go tonight?"

"There is a performance in half an hour, my pet. We shall just catch it."

"A perfect place to play our little game, Papa. I shall instruct you on the way. Eat your oysters—you will need them!"

All things do not always turn our way. The "club" was less than our imaginations had built up. The "paintings" turned out to be no more or less than crude representations of the true masters of the palette. The stage was tawdry and the set pieces even more so. Where we sought beauty in the females—unclothed for the most part as they were each time the ragged curtains drew back—we found only gaucheness and unpleasing limbs.

The seats were no more than wooden chairs. The audience numbered perhaps fifteen. I was groped frequently in the darkness. Perhaps it was my mood. A little more luxury or comfort would have turned it. The audible thwacks of naked bellies on the stage and the visible entering of pricks stirred me little.

"Papa, we will go."

He needed but my request. Eyes stared curiously after us in our exit.

"I prefer elegance, Papa. Lewdness itself is not enough."

"I agree."

In the darkness of the carriage that returned us to our hotel our lips met. I thought of the first time we had ever driven so, in Hyde Park, shortly after my return from finishing school. Papa's hand had for the first time strayed within my corsage then. It did now. I assisted the movement. His fingertips, thrust down within the tight bodice, brushed my nipples.

"You prefer more accustomed surroundings nowadays, Eveline."

"Excitement, Papa. The stage scenes were enacted with coldness as if they were mechanical beings. Indeed, they looked it. And the girls' legs were grubby. How horrid!"

I laughed despite myself. I had sounded prudish. Perhaps my ways were changing, though not my desires.

"Careful, Papa—we are almost there."

His hand withdrew itself, leaving my nipples tingling. In order to conceal his own excitement he was forced to hold his top hat in front of him as we ascended from the cab. Papa paid the man. We entered. The red velvet couches, the polished wood, and the etched glass screens in the foyer were a balm after the crudities of the so-called *Théâtre Érotique*.

A woman in passing across the foyer stopped of a sudden and stared. Her gown was of the finest, her hat prettily decorated with boa feathers and imitation cherries.

"Maude!"

"Edward!"

Despite the fondness of their greeting, which was accompanied by several kisses on the cheeks, Papa looked dumbfounded, as well he might. An old, dear friend, he began to explain while Maude—or Lady Drisdale, as in fact she was—turned to me with a huge smile.

"This surely must be Eveline! Indeed, I can see the likeness!"

"Yes," I replied simply. To be undone is to be undone, though with a certain alacrity Papa came to the aid of the situation. Casting a quick glance about him lest any further names be mentioned, he succeeded in taking her with us to the glass-fronted lift. Hurried explanations followed. Papa was on a secret diplomatic mission, he said. It was imperative that no one knew his true identity.

"Oh, my dear, I would not wish to spoil anything! Come to my suite. Let us celebrate our meeting at least. I will have some champagne brought up."

Her eyes quite sparkled as she spoke. She was in her late thirties and carried as appealing a figure as anyone might wish to see. As befitted my supposed demeanour I said little. I had yet to gauge her properly. Papa seemed to have done so only too well. He threw me several glances as we entered the suite. He seemed a trifle excited.

We cast off our cloaks and bonnets. Champagne was quickly served. Questions and reminiscences rattled back and forth. Now and then I was the recipient of her looks. She had separated from her husband, so she prattled. She was a free woman, though she had a companion—a very young man as she described him.

"I am teaching him French, but only the naughty words. Do you know any naughty words in French, Eveline?"

I shook my head. I was mute. I would have brought a blush to my cheeks if I could. My attitude seemed to please rather than disconcert her. A knock sounded as we were imbibing our second glasses. The young man appeared. His name was Rupert. His voice betokened that he came of good family. He looked about seventeen and was quiet and pale.

"Edward, you must get acquainted with this young man. Perhaps you would like to smoke? Eveline and I will retire while you do. Eveline, be a dear girl and bring our glasses. I will bring the other bottle."

My astonishment was considerable. The boudoir beyond the drawing room was ornate and luxurious.

"Do you like it? I always have this suite—it is their very

best. And do you not love Paris, Eveline? It is so deliciously naughty, don't you think?"

"Mama has always said I must never be naughty."

"Come, sit upon the bed with me—it is much more comfortable. Drink your champagne. Naughty is as naughty does, you know."

"Oh, but the bubbles tickle my nose so! Oh, and your hand does, too!"

Unbidden, her fingers had strayed so far beneath the hem of my gown that already they encountered my garters. I opened my mouth in astonishment, or indeed in such a pretence of it that she was well deceived. I fell back. The champagne spilled from its glass.

"There! you have wet your dress! Come let me help you take it off, Eveline—or may I call you Evie?"

"No—yes—oh, what are you doing? Pray do not touch me there! I shall call Papa!"

I wriggled, I squirmed. Her hand had sought my nest. It tickled divinely. I arched my back. My gown was indeed wet. The glass, half full, had fallen. A forefinger as artless as I have ever known sought and found my button. Her lips encountered my own. I gave a fine pretence of fluttering.

"Pray do not! It is naughty!"

"It is lovely, Evie. Has your little garden not been watered yet?"

"OH! you are making me feel funny! Please stop! OH!"

I bubbled, I gasped. The actress in me came to the fore. By deliberately rolling about and giving all pretence of evading the tongue which had by now tasted my own, I permitted her to unbutton my gown.

"Oh, what are you at? Papa will see me if he comes in!"

"What treasures! What delicious firm breasts, what lovely legs you have. Has he not yet seen it all?"

"Oh! how horrid you are! You will have me naked in a moment! Dear Papa will be shocked!"

A delicious wrestling ensued during which by effecting a resistance I caused her own gown to be swept up. Like myself she wore no drawers. Her thighs were sumptuous. Our garters rubbed together. I sobbed, I squirmed. Finally, as it seemed to her, I was overcome. My nipples had risen beneath the titillation of her lips. Inert and panting I lay, her hand cupped beneath my moist slit. I pretended small petulant cries while succumbing ever more to her kisses. Seeing me thus at last, she rose and quickly divested herself of her gown. But for her stockings—black to my white—she was as naked as I. She rolled upon me.

"Let me excite you, Evie—I can, I shall. Oh, the wicked things I shall make you do! How long I have waited for this!"

"Waited?"

"Since you were fifteen, my pet—before you left for the *pensionnat* just outside Paris. I admired you from a distance. I swore one day to kiss your cherry lips, and more!"

"OH! how funny you make me feel! More? What can be more?"

"Your dear Papa was there, as I. His eyes never left you. His sighs were such as told me the whole story. His prick stiffened at the very sight of you. Did you know it not?"

With every word her silken belly rubbed suavely upon mine. I was beside myself with desire, yet could not fully show it. A haunted gaze as of one torn between excitement and disbelief lay in my eyes.

"Papa? Oh, stop, you are driving me mad! Such things cannot be true—they cannot! Oh! the way you rub your thing against mine!"

"Yes—isn't it nice! I knew you would like it. Would you

like something else there now, Evie—something thick and long?"

"I cannot! I dare not! Oh, what is this you speak of? Let me up!"

She laughed—a laugh as truly victorious as any I have heard. Raising her head while holding me pinned beneath her, my legs forced open by her feet which had hooked inside my ankles, she called Papa's name.

I shrieked—though not so loudly as might have alerted any in the nearby rooms. Papa entered in a second. His look of astonishment was profound.

"Eveline!"

"Papa! OH! Oh, do not let him see me thus!"

"Quickly, Edward, she is ready for it!"

"My God, do I dare! How luscious she looks—what dazzling curves!"

Dare indeed he did, for in but a moment he was stripped. A further scream escaped me. Maude's hand covered over my mouth. She rolled from me. I bucked and made as if to rise.

"Oh, Mama!"

"Lie still, Evie! See how he wants you! What a prick he has!"

I yelled, I kicked. Maude held my shoulders. Even Papa perhaps was taken aback by the vehemence of my acting. The subtle movements of my legs assisted him. Twisting my face wildly beneath the hand of Maude, I felt the knob insert. Had she but known it I was almost spilling already in my excitement.

"No, Papa! OH!"

My mouth had escaped her hand only to be muffled beneath his. I shot my tongue into his mouth. His cock slid in me to the full. I bucked, I yammered.

"Maude, how tight she is, how delicious! Come, Eveline, give it to me! Ah, how I have waited for this!"

"You mustn't, Papa! Stop! OH! it is right in me—it's too big!"

Puffing and panting and ensuring by every possible means that the wriggling of my bottom allowed him to piston me to the full, our bout began. Interspersing it as I did with sobs and cries, Maude could never have been more convinced. Choosing the moment, I bubbled out my halting words of acquiescence at last. Under Maude's "tuition" I raised my white-stockinged legs and passed them over his buttocks. I pouted, I sobbed, I drummed with my heels. All too soon I was inundated with as thick a pool of sperm as I had ever received. My cries of pleasure might well have been taken by Maude for anguish.

Drawing me from beneath my victor, she cosseted and cuddled me, passing her hand down between my thighs for sticky proof of my fulfillment. Suffice to say that I had not forgotten the distant presence of Rupert, who was then called. Nor had I forgotten the behaviour of Emma. I screeched. I hid myself beneath the sheet. I veiled my eyes.

Nought availed. Undressing, Rupert offered to my view a penis long and slender.

"Oh no! I cannot! Have you not made me naughty enough!"

"What nonsense, Eveline, you will enjoy them both. You are old enough for all such pleasures now!"

How well I simulated coyness while bumping my bottom luringly against Papa! His penis stirred. Sandwiched between the two I was placed upon him. Presenting himself anew to my bedewed lovelips, he entered his thick shaft with majestic slowness. Such a tremor of lewdness seized us that I could scarce disguise my features as all sank up within me. I gripped, I squirmed.

"Stop it! Don't let him! Not Rupert, too!"

Maude seized my neck. 'Tis ever the best grip to subdue. A gentle smack on my bottom and the split globe was offered, drawing me half off of Papa's throbbing pleasure. I moaned, I gasped. A long whimper escaped me as the second was presented. Its knob urged against my rosehole. Such were my pretended cries that Papa was forced to hold me firmly.

I shrieked, I bit his shoulder as the more slender lance of Rupert entered. I felt its passage inch by inch.

"Oh no, I cannot! Papa! Rupert! Stop!"

The rest became but a haze of desire. Such sobs of mine as filled the boudoir spoke only of the wanton madness into which we had entered. The lascivious tableau we must have presented would have stirred a statue. With hollow groans both at last expelled their tributes within me while, as for Papa's prick, it was duly soaked with my spendings. In Maude's eyes the conversion of her "pupil" was complete. I pride myself that I played my role to perfection.

Casting my satiated body into my own bed close to dawn, I slept until eleven and then enjoyed a late breakfast with Papa.

"Was it intended—plotted, Papa? Come, you must tell me. I forgive all."

"By no means, my darling. Maude is an actress who married into Society. She was ever a wild one, but I had not expected this. Even so, when she introduced Rupert and led you into the bedroom, I knew what to expect. At any moment, she may descend to breakfast, too. Do you wish to encounter her again?"

"No, Papa, I think we will make haste and leave. Paris is unlikely to be able to match the events of the night."

"I pray we may be able to rely on her discretion, Eveline."

"Have no fear on it, Papa. She will treasure the secret as much as she enjoyed bringing it about."

I was proved right. Months later in London I encountered Maude at a ball. She advanced towards me smiling.

"Forgive me—are you not the daughter of Lord L.? Permit me to introduce myself—I have been longing to meet you."

We chatted agreeably. Companions joined us. None would have guessed at what we knew. In parting, Maude gave me a wink. Though deeming it, as I have said before, a common gesture, I returned it. Our paths were not to cross again except formally. Society—experiencing yet another crack in its hypocritical facade—would have pretended horror.

Returning from that selfsame ball with Papa and in the company also of Sir Langham Beamish, I remarked with great innocence: "Who are all those girls who parade nightly in the Haymarket, Papa?"

Papa assumed a frown. He hesitated, it seemed, to reply. Sir Langham leaned forward. In doing so his hand brushed my knee.

"They are fallen women, Eveline. Gay girls, as they are wrongfully called. I fear to tell you that they sell their favours nightly to all who can pay for them."

"Oh! how horrid! I wish I had not asked. Pray forgive me!"

"No matter, Eveline. In your innocence you could never have known. It is best, however, to learn something of the ways of the world."

"Yes, Papa."

I squeezed his hand as if seeking reassurance. Sir Langham Beamish beamed at me kindly.

Our carriage rattled on.

MORE EROTIC CLASSICS FROM CARROLL & GRAF

☐ Anonymous/ALTAR OF VENUS $3.95
☐ Anonymous/AUTOBIOGRAPHY OF A FLEA $3.95
☐ Anonymous/THE CELEBRATED MISTRESS $3.95
☐ Anonymous/CONFESSIONS OF AN ENGLISH MAID $3.95
☐ Anonymous/CONFESSIONS OF EVELINE $3.95
☐ Anonymous/COURT OF VENUS $3.95
☐ Anonymous/DANGEROUS AFFAIRS $3.95
☐ Anonymous/THE DIARY OF MATA HARI $3.95
☐ Anonymous/DOLLY MORTON $3.95
☐ Anonymous/THE EDUCATION OF A MAIDEN $3.95
☐ Anonymous/THE EROTIC READER $3.95
☐ Anonymous/THE EROTIC READER II $3.95
☐ Anonymous/THE EROTIC READER III $4.50
☐ Anonymous/FANNY HILL'S DAUGHTER $3.95
☐ Anonymous/FLORENTINE AND JULIA $3.95
☐ Anonymous/A LADY OF QUALITY $3.95
☐ Anonymous/LENA'S STORY $3.95
☐ Anonymous/THE LIBERTINES $4.50
☐ Anonymous/LOVE PAGODA $3.95
☐ Anonymous/THE LUSTFUL TURK $3.95
☐ Anonymous/MADELEINE $3.95
☐ Anonymous/A MAID'S JOURNEY $3.95
☐ Anonymous/MAID'S NIGHT IN $3.95
☐ Anonymous/THE OYSTER $3.95
☐ Anonymous/THE OYSTER II $3.95
☐ Anonymous/THE OYSTER III $4.50
☐ Anonymous/PARISIAN NIGHTS $4.50
☐ Anonymous/PLEASURES AND FOLLIES $3.95
☐ Anonymous/PLEASURE'S MISTRESS $3.95
☐ Anonymous/PRIMA DONNA $3.95
☐ Anonymous/ROSA FIELDING: VICTIM OF LUST $3.95
☐ Anonymous/SATANIC VENUS $4.50
☐ Anonymous/SECRET LIVES $3.95
☐ Anonymous/THREE TIMES A WOMAN $3.95

☐	Anonymous/VENUS DISPOSES	$3.95
☐	Anonymous/VENUS IN PARIS	$3.95
☐	Anonymous/VENUS UNBOUND	$3.95
☐	Anonymous/VENUS UNMASKED	$3.95
☐	Anonymous/VICTORIAN FANCIES	$3.95
☐	Anonymous/THE WANTONS	$3.95
☐	Anonymous/A WOMAN OF PLEASURE	$3.95
☐	Anonymous/WHITE THIGHS	$4.50
☐	Perez, Faustino/LA LOLITA	$3.95
☐	van Heller, Marcus/ADAM & EVE	$3.95
☐	van Heller, Marcus/THE FRENCH WAY	$3.95
☐	van Heller, Marcus/THE HOUSE OF BORGIA	$3.95
☐	van Heller, Marcus/THE LOINS OF AMON	$3.95
☐	van Heller, Marcus/ROMAN ORGY	$3.95
☐	van Heller, Marcus/VENUS IN LACE	$3.95
☐	Villefranche, Anne-Marie/FOLIES D'AMOUR	$3.95
	Cloth	$14.95
☐	Villefranche, Anne-Marie/JOIE D'AMOUR	$3.95
	Cloth	$13.95
☐	Villefranche, Anne-Marie/ MYSTERE D'AMOUR	$3.95
☐	Villefranche, Anne-Marie/PLAISIR D'AMOUR	$3.95
	Cloth	$12.95
☐	Von Falkensee, Margarete/BLUE ANGEL NIGHTS	$3.95
☐	Von Falkensee, Margarete/BLUE ANGEL SECRETS	$4.50

Available from fine bookstores everywhere or use this coupon for ordering.

Carroll & Graf Publishers, Inc., 260 Fifth Avenue, N.Y., N.Y. 10001

Please send me the books I have checked above. I am enclosing $_____ (please add $1.00 per title to cover postage and handling.) Send check or money order—no cash or C.O.D.'s please. N.Y. residents please add 8¼% sales tax.

Mr/Mrs/Ms _____
Address _____
City _____ State/Zip _____
Please allow four to six weeks for delivery.